THE RISK TAKER

CATHRYN FOX

COPYRIGHT

Discover other titles by Cathryn Fox at www.cathrynfox.com. Please sign up for Cathryn's Newsletter for freebies, ebooks, news and contests:

https://app.mailerlite.com/webforms/landing/c1f8n1

ISBN ebook 978-1-928056-99-7
Print: 978-1-989374-00-9

FALLON

I take a huge breath and slowly ease my foot off the gas pedal to coast my SUV into the long winding driveway. A quick glance in my rearview mirror reveals my son, still sound asleep in his car seat, and my heart wobbles as he mumbles something incoherent in his slumber.

My gaze rakes over him, takes in his mess of dark hair, sun-kissed skin and plump rosy lips. Honest to God, with each passing day he looks more and more like his father. But thinking of my late husband Ethan has my heart punching into my throat, forcing me to once again fight back the tears at his senseless, tragic death.

I turn my attention back to the house rising up before me. I haven't been back to Seattle since the car accident that killed Ethan, as well as Sara's unborn baby—Sara was engaged to Ethan's brother Jamie, and was to become my sister in law. The four of us were close, but after the funeral, Sara left Jamie, and I needed time away.

With hardly any belongings, I hopped into my vehicle and took three-year-old Chase to my Mom's house in Spokane to grieve in my childhood home. But it's been a little more than a year and it's time I got back into the work force, and start walking amongst the living again. Chase is four years old now and he needs stability, pre-school, and most importantly, a strong male influence in his life. That's where my late husband's brother Jamie comes in. At least that's what I'm hoping for. He sort of fell off the grid after hockey season ended a few months ago and has stopped answering my calls or returning my texts. Jamie and I were always close, the best of friends. He was there for me when Ethan traveled, so his silence, his disappearance from my life, has left a gaping hole —in so many ways.

I kill the ignition, and Chase stirs in his seat. "Mommy," he whines, and I unbuckle myself.

"We're here," I say quietly, but have no idea if he remembers the house we once lived in, the place where he was conceived, and where we made memories for three special years.

He rubs his tired eyes with his knuckles. "I'm thirsty."

"I'll get you a drink as soon as we get inside."

I exit the car, and the warm night air falls over me as I open his door. When we left here a year ago, we fled with only our luggage. I'd left everything behind, the house and contents, unable to deal with the reality of the situation. I unbuckle Chase and, dinky car in hand, he jumps from his car seat onto the concrete driveway. The lights in his sneakers flash as he lands with a thud on two feet.

Since it's way past his bedtime, I say, "After your drink, I'll tuck you into your race car bed and you can go back to sleep." I pause for a moment, gauge his face for recognition, and my heart stalls when I see it.

His big brown eyes go wide when he lifts his chin to sees the house. He blinks once, then twice, like he's trying to gather his bearings. "Is Daddy here?" he asks, and I unsuccessfully try to choke down the garbled sounds rising up in my throat. A street light flickers overhead as I drop to my knees, and put my hands on his shoulders.

"Daddy is in heaven, remember, Chase?"

He glances up into the dark night sky, a black canvas shimmering with a mosaic of stars. He points. "Up there."

"That's right. He's watching us from up there."

Keep it together, Fallon.

"I want Daddy here," he pouts, and I fight the tears.

Things might not have been perfect between Ethan and me, but he was a good father when he was home, and Chase treasured their time together. Until...

Until the fearless, no holds barred NASCAR racer who could handle any vehicle ended up driving his own over a guardrail. Unbelievable really. There are still so many unanswered questions, and while I have my own theory on what happened that day, well...I can't bring myself to seek the truth, or even vocalize my thoughts. Can't bring myself to charge Ethan's phone, and read his last texts, ones that could either confirm or disprove my suspicions. Either way, it won't bring Ethan back. Won't bring back the guy who was wild and reckless, and at times thought he was invincible.

He wasn't.

"Let's go inside and get you a drink," I say, in my best cheerful voice.

I scoop him up, and since I have no groceries, grab the cooler bag from the back seat and head to the front door. Memories bombard me and my chest constricts as I insert my key and open the door to our house, now quiet, dark...lifeless. A stale scent drifts by my nose, and I almost can't breathe as I glance at the sofa, lit by the streetlight slanting in through the big bay window, and find Ethan's favorite spot empty. But for Chase's sake, I need to keep myself together. Tonight, when he's sound asleep, I'll snuggle up with a bottle of wine, and weep quietly for a young man taken from this earth far too early, and for a little boy who will grow up without a father. I really hope Jamie comes through for him, because I have no plans or desire to date—now or ever. Marriage isn't in my future and right now, my son needs all my focus. Besides that, I'm in no state, mental or physical, to put myself out there again. I haven't even lost the baby weight. If I had, maybe Ethan wouldn't have...

I cut off those thoughts, unable to go down that road as I hold Chase against me, and shut and lock the front door. Sliding my hand along the wall, I find the switch and we both blink when the bright white light floods the entryway. I take in my once cozy place, but I'll never think of this house as home sweet home again.

Chase wiggles in my arms and I set him down. Dinky car still held tight in one hand, he reaches into the cooler bag and pulls out his juice box and some crackers. I step further into the house and a bang at the back patio door startles me. My hand flies to my chest and I gasp. Another bang sounds, almost like the lid of a barbecue being slammed shut, or a garbage can being tipped over.

Could it be an animal? The place has been abandoned for a long time. Maybe Jamie hasn't been looking after it like he once assured me he would.

"Chase, I want you to stay right here, okay?" I point to the floor. "Don't move from this spot."

"Okay," he says and stuffs his face full of crackers.

I slowly open the front hall closet and feel a measure of relief when I come across Ethan's old baseball bat. I scoop it up, weight it in my hand and walk toward the patio door. I check the lock, find it secure. With a flick of the switch, the backyard lights up, and showcases very neglected foliage and a pool full of dirt and algae. The click of the lock sounds like a gun being cocked as I open the door and step out, bat poised on my shoulder. As a nurse, we've taken self-defense courses to help us deal with unruly people, but I'm not sure I could actually hit someone with a bat.

Please be an animal.

I glance toward the barbecue and before I know what's happening, someone has me by the front of my T-shirt and is shoving me against the side of the house. My head hits with a thud and I wince and shut my eyes as stars dance before them.

"Take what you want," I say, my thoughts focused solely on protecting my son. He's all that matters. TVs and computers, phones and jewelry, they mean nothing in the big scheme of things.

"Fallon?"

My eyes blink open at the familiar voice and I cry out in relief when I find Jamie looming over me. "Oh, God, Jamie. You scared me."

"What the hell, Fallon?" His dark eyes narrow in on me, his gaze roaming my face. "What are you doing?"

He takes the baseball bat from me, runs his fingers through his too long hair and backs up. As I work to gather myself, my gaze races over the long length of him. My Lord, what happened to him since I've been gone? He used to keep his hair neat and short, now it's longer than usual and hanging in his eyes. The clothes on his back look like they've been doubling as his pajamas for a week straight, and the beer on his breath is enough to spike my blood alcohol levels.

"I thought you were an intruder...or an animal," I say, still breathless.

"I was just checking on the place," he informs me in a gruff voice, like he's angry with me. "I told you I would," he snaps.

I jerk my thumb over my shoulder. "I didn't see your car. It wasn't in the driveway." Which is a good thing, considering he's been drinking. The last thing I want is for him to be taken to the hospital because of a car accident—one fatality from driving is enough for any family. Or should I say two, considering the unborn baby.

He rakes an unsteady hand through his hair and shakes his head. "I live two houses down or did you forget?"

"No, I didn't forget."

"I could..." He stops to swallow. "There's been a string of break-ins in the neighborhood lately. I could have hurt you." There is real fear in his eyes when they meet mine and that's when I understand where his anger is coming from. He was worried about me, and in his current state could have reacted first, asked questions later.

"I texted to let you know I was coming back," I explain. "Didn't you get it?"

"I got it," he grumbles.

Knowing he was purposely ignoring me widens the gaping hole inside me.

"I just came a bit earlier, is all."

He waves his hands. "Which is why I thought I had more time."

I try to figure out what he's waving at. "For what?"

"To get this place cleaned up for you." His throat makes a sound as he swallows again. "I kind of just let it go. I didn't want...you don't deserve...Ethan would have..."

"Mommy..."

I spin around fast, and Chase is staring up at us. His big brown eyes, so similar to his father's, and to his uncle's, are confused, a bit frightened as he grips his dinky car.

"Chase," I say quickly, and hurry to him. "Do you remember Uncle Jamie?"

"I don't know," he says. Chase was young, and the car accident happened just after hockey season ended, and Jamie had been away a lot that year. But on some level, deep inside the little boy, I suspect he has some buried memories of the man looming close.

I smile at my perplexed son. "Well, why don't you say hello. You're going to really like Uncle Jamie."

"Hello," he says, tilting his head back and moving closer to my leg.

"Hi Chase," Jamie says, and takes a distancing step backward. What the hell? Is he afraid of his nephew? He might have been absent a lot that last year, but when Jamie was around in the summer, he was definitely the fun uncle. But when my gaze meets his, sees the pain in the shadowy depths, I understand completely. Looking at Chase must be like a punch to the gut, considering he's the spitting image of Ethan when he was the same age.

As the oldest brother by three years, Jamie would have remembered Ethan at the age of four, remembered every trait and nuance. Ethan had told me Jamie was always a good big brother, and I guess that's why Ethan's jealousy always confused me. Oh, he'd never come right out and say mean things, but I felt there was a hint of anger in the joking jibes spoken behind his brother's back. It always seemed like Ethan wanted what Jamie had, and always wanted to outshine him.

But despite it all they were brothers and Jamie always looked out for his wild, reckless younger sibling, even though Jamie was known to be a risk taker too. Hence his hockey name. As I look at him now, however, I don't get the sense he's a guy whose about to risk anything. Not anymore. A loss will make you more cautious. That I know first-hand.

A dog barks in the distance and snaps me back to attention. "Let's get inside." I usher Chase in and Jamie follows. I walk around and flick all the lights on, like that will somehow chase away the ghosts that haunt me.

Chase climbs into the chair at the table, and makes noises

as he runs his dinky car over the tabletop. I open and close the cupboards and fridge. I find a few canned goods, that have long ago expired, and set them on the counter to dispose of.

"I cleaned out the fridge, donated a bunch of canned goods last Christmas," Jamie says, his voice quiet.

"Thanks, Jamie. I hate to see good food go to waste."

"Are you hungry? I could order a pizza, or we could go to my place and I could make you something. I'm not a great cook, but I can get by."

My stomach takes that moment to grumble. "Actually, a pizza sounds good."

"Mario's," we both say at the same time and Jamie gives me the first smile of the night. It brightens his face, and reminds me of the once handsome, carefree guy from years ago. But I'm not so sure he exists anymore. We've both have gone through a lot since the accident. It was his pregnant fiancée in the car with my husband, and she walked away from Jamie after she lost the baby. I want to ask if he's heard from her, but don't want to open old wounds. Rumor has it he's been with a lot of puck bunnies since Sara, but who am I to judge. We all grieve differently.

He pulls his phone from his pocket and punches in a number.

"Mommy, I want pizza."

"Okay," I say, knowing I'm going to regret feeding him pizza this late at night. He'd eaten on the drive here, but I'm not going to deny him a slice. "Can you get a cheese and pepperoni for Chase?"

Dark brown eyes so similar to Chase's move over my face. "Pizza with the works okay for you?"

"Same as always," I say, then go perfectly still. Nothing is the same as always. Why would I even say that? Oh, maybe because being in this house again, surrounded by all things

Ethan is messing with me hard. I lean against the archway, and glance into the dining room. My gaze flickers over the framed wedding photo, as well as the photo of us holding Chase for the first time, and that's when it really hits me.

I can't stay here.

A big, heavy hand lands on my shoulder and I jump a good foot in the air. I turn, and Jamie pulls me into his arms. "Sorry, didn't mean to scare you." He holds me tight, and my throat aches. It feels so good to be held, hugged—by him. He slowly inches back, and his eyes meet mine again. "Are you okay?"

"No, Jamie. I'm not okay. I'll probably never be okay again."

"Me neither," he says, and slides his hand around my head to lay it against his pounding heart, which is just as shattered as mine.

Will we ever be able to put the pieces back together again? Find some semblance of a life?

Will either of us ever be able to find normal?

2

JAMIE

Here I thought I'd been doing okay until I set eyes on Fallon. Then again, who am I kidding? I've not been doing okay for a very long time. But the second I looked into Fallon's eyes, every painful memory of Sara losing the baby and leaving me, and my kid brother being rushed to the hospital only to die on the way, came crashing back in a whoosh.

Jesus Christ, I'll never forgive myself for any of it.

How could I?

I was supposed to be the one taking Sara to her appointment. She trusted in me to get her there, and I let her down. Trust is so important to me and I totally fucked up. The damn practice went into overtime, and then we had a field of puck bunnies to push our way through. Sara had obviously turned to Ethan, could trust in my younger brother when she couldn't trust in me, and now he's dead, our baby is gone, and Sara fled the state, never to be heard from again. Yeah, all that is my fault and I don't deserve to ever be okay again.

Fuck man, I still have no idea what happened that day. The roads were dry and clear, and Ethan was the best driver I knew. Reports came back that there was nothing wrong with the car, and the single vehicle accident was driver error. Here it is a year later, and I'm still having a hard time wrapping my brain around one of the world's best NASCAR drivers crashing through a guardrail.

"Jamie?"

I blink and realize Fallon had been talking to me. Dammit. I need to stop spacing out. Once again, I had one too many beers tonight, a habit I've fallen into when I'm home alone, haunted by memories. I can still picture Sara glaring at me with angry eyes, telling me it was all my fault. A guy doesn't move past that easily, or ever.

"Sorry, what?"

Her brow furrows and her look is one of pity that I fucking hate. I'm a horrible person, a complete fuck up, and I don't deserve compassion or sympathy from anyone, least of all Fallon. By rights she should hate me. She should kick me in the nuts and call me every vile name known to mankind. But no, sweet Fallon isn't at all like that. My sister-in-law is the kindest woman I know and always put others above herself. I knew that from the second my brother and I laid eyes on her at her girlfriend's party all those years ago. Hell, back in the day, if Ethan hadn't put a ring on her finger, maybe things would have been different between us.

Or maybe not, since I was on the road so much, making a name for myself in the NHL. While I was away working my ass off in the rink, he swooped in and made her his girl. Eventually I met Sara. A nice girl and one of the team's physical therapists. She got pregnant, despite the fact that I always used protection, but sometimes things happen. Condoms aren't one-hundred percent effective. Obviously. At the time, all my friends were getting married, and having kids, and when she showed me the pregnancy stick, I knew it was time for me to grow up too, and do the right thing.

"I was just wondering if you'd like a drink," she says pulling my thoughts back once again.

"Yeah, sure," I say and as I gaze at her, take in her strength and her vulnerability, my heart hitches. Truthfully, I would do anything for her, and goddammit, I should have had the place cleaned and stocked for her and Chase. Once again, I let down those who counted on me. It's no wonder Fallon ran away from here so fast after the funerals. I guess she knew better than to turn to me.

"I don't have any beer, but I have some soda. Would you like one?"

"I think I'm done with drinking tonight anyway," I say. Maybe forever. I glance at the young boy at the table. While my risk-taking days are behind me, and I'm never going to be what these two need—I can't let anyone get too close, can't let anyone rely on me—I should at least be sober around him. Ethan would want that.

"Would you keep an eye on Chase for a second? I'll grab them from the SUV."

I hold my hand out. "Give me your keys. I'll bring all your stuff in."

"There isn't much." She reaches into her pocket and pulls out her keys. "We only have our clothes."

"Yeah, you didn't take much of anything when you left," I say and close my hand around the palm tree keychain that says Margaritaville—a souvenir she'd picked up on her honeymoon in Jamaica. I make my way to the front door and the warm night air washes over me. The sight of the SUV in the driveway is like a kick in the nuts. I was with them when they bought it. Checked out the back seat with my nephew.

I open the back hatch and pull out their things as well as a paper grocery bag with soda and chips. Was this supposed to be her dinner? Guess she's been eating about as well as I have. I gather up what little belongings she has and carry everything inside. I step into the kitchen and find Fallon staring off in to space.

"I'll take these upstairs," I say. I pause. "Um..." I begin not sure how to ask, but she comes to my rescue because she's a smart girl who is good at reading people and situations.

"I think I'm going to sleep in the spare room."

I nod, figuring as much.

"Chase okay in his room?"

"Yes, I think he'll like crawling back into his race car bed."

I glance at the boy who is the spitting image of his father. I focus back in on Fallon and lower my voice. "Does he...remember?"

"A little bit," she says and pulls the soda from the bag. I turn and go upstairs. I've been keeping an eye on the place for some time now, so this isn't my first trip to the bedrooms after Fallon left. Still, seeing the open closet, with Ethan's clothes hanging, a shelf with all his favorite ball caps, hits like a punch every single time.

Since Fallon didn't say which spare room, I drop her bag into the one across the hall from Chase's, and set his stuff on the floor of his room, near the foot of his hot rod racecar bed, similar to the one his daddy drove.

I take a fueling breath and head back downstairs. My cell pings and I pull it from my back pocket to read a text from Rider. He and Kane are shooting a game of pool at the Freeman's bar. They've both been keeping a close eye on me over the last year—Heck, all the guys and their wives have been— and while I'd normally join them, go home with a puck bunny, tonight I'm not in the mood. I swipe my finger over the phone and send a text.

Jamie: Fallon is back. I'm with her and Chase at her house.

Rider: Fallon Adams? Your sister-in-law?

Jamie: Do you know any other Fallon who has a son named Chase?

Rider: You okay, buddy?

Jamie: As well as could be expected.

Rider: Wants some company. Kane and I can come over.

Jamie: Nah, I'm good. Having pizza and then crashing.

Rider: Say hi to Fallon for us.

Jamie: Will do.

I shove the phone back into my pocket and step into the kitchen. "That was Rider."

She hands me a soda and I take a big drink. "If I'm keeping you from something."

"No, you're not and the guys say hi."

She nods. "How are they doing?"

"Same," I say with a shrug.

"Rider still the Wing Man?" she asks with a small grin.

I snort. "You remember that?"

"I spent hours listening to him build his teammates up to the girls, but it's time he realizes his value and shows a woman who he is, not who his friends are."

"You always liked him, didn't you?"

Her smile is soft, like she's remembering happier times. "He was always nice to me, and he adored Chase."

I nod. "Too bad he's a sworn bachelor."

She gives me a teasing wink. "I'm pretty sure I once heard you say that, and look what..." She lets her words fall off, and her eyes go wide, like she's said too much. But just then the doorbell rings, and cuts the quiet.

"Pizza," I say happy for the distraction. I pull a few bills from my pocket and head to the door. I hand the money over and take the pizza. Fallon is setting out plates when I get back. She has a worried look on her face as I open the boxes and put a slice on each plate.

"Pizza," Chase yells and rubs his sleepy eyes. I grin at him and rustle his hair. He kind of reminds me of myself as a kid. I'd fight sleep any day for food. Still would.

I take a seat, bite into my slice, and study Fallon's body language. She's wound so tight, her damn shoulders are practically hugging her ears. "What's on your mind?" I ask.

She smiles at me. "You always could read me."

"You're the one who's good at reading others and situations."

"Comes with being a nurse."

I nod. "I can only read you because we used to spend a lot of time together."

"True, we did. You were always there in the summers when Ethan was away," she says. "We did a lot of things together before Chase was born," she adds, but then she swallows, and her eyes slowly lift to mine. "I don't think I can stay here, Jamie."

"You can stay with me for as long as it takes," I say quickly, and without thinking. I'm not about to abandon her, and while I can let her into my house, I can't let her or anyone into my heart, can't let her think she can count on me.

"No, what I mean is, I have to sell this place." She waves her hand around. "It's too big for just Chase and me."

What she's not saying is that she and Ethan had planned to fill all those spare bedrooms, and this place has too many memories.

"Yeah, I get that. My place is too big too, but I bought it to be close to you guys." I bite into my slice, chew, and swallow it down with a drink of soda. I used to love hanging out here, and my ex Sara and Fallon had become good friends. Fallon was going to be Sara's matron of honor, and naturally Ethan would have been my best man. But that's all in the past now.

"Do you know any good realtors?" she asks and lets loose a big sigh.

"I can ask around. My mom probably does. They downsized after..." I don't need to finish the sentence for Fallon to realize they were unable to stay in the house they'd raised Ethan in after he'd died.

"I need to go see them. I feel bad for being away so long. It wasn't fair for me to run away without considering their feelings."

"They will love that, but they knew you needed space. I can take you tomorrow if you want. You can talk to Mom about a realtor."

"Thanks, Jamie."

Christ, what is it about her saying 'thanks, Jamie' that hits like a fist and has me wanting to do more—everything—for her? Why does it make me want to pull her to me, and chase away all her bad memories in the bedroom?

Whoa shit, don't go there, buddy.

She lets loose another heavy sigh. "I'm going to have to stage the place."

I point to the pizza. "Another slice?"

Her look is almost embarrassed as she puts her hand over her stomach and says, "I probably shouldn't."

What the hell?

"Why not?" I question.

"Well, my metabolism isn't the same as before I had Chase."

I take that moment to let my gaze take her in, admiring every single inch, from the tip of her head to toes that are curling beneath her. Her long, honey blonde hair is piled haphazardly in a flimsy clip. Many loose strands fall teasingly over her cheeks, and shoulders. My attention drops from her face to her body, to admire her smooth, creamy skin, and plump breasts that are straining behind her Seattle Seahawks

T-shirt. She always was a football fan over hockey, but that never stopped her from watching all my games. I turn my attention to yoga pants that showcase plump hips any man would long to sink his teeth into and strong, well-shaped legs that have carried her along in the hardest of situations. Everything about her is beautiful, and admirable. She squirms, uncomfortable under my scrutiny.

"You're perfect," I mumble.

I swallow a moan, and berate myself. Shit, she's always been breathtaking, and the extra weight, which emphasizes all her sexy curves, looks good on her. Damn, good on her. But what the fuck am I doing? The last person I should be admiring or having inappropriate thoughts about is my sister-in-law, no matter what I've always felt about her. No, it's best I stick to puck bunnies. No history. No commitment. No tomorrows.

No pain.

"You can hire out for staging," I point out, changing the subject before I say or do something stupid.

"Yeah, but I have to deal..."

I lift my head, and drop the rest of my pizza onto my plate, as Chase grows restless in his chair. "I can clear his things out. Donate what I can. Just let me know what you want to keep. I can do that for you, Fallon. I would have done it already, but I just didn't want to overstep here."

"I can't ask you to. It's not easy for you, either."

No, but I don't want easy. I don't deserve it. "Consider it done."

"I'll take a few keepsakes." She nods and picks a piece of bacon off her pizza and looks a million miles away as she pops it into her mouth. "I'd like to enroll Chase in pre-school a few days a week this summer. I think the interaction would be good for him, and he's going to need to make friends. Plus, I plan on going back to work."

"Really?" I ask, surprised. She doesn't need the money, but maybe she needs work to find herself again. I needed my hockey. Would have been lost without it.

"Yeah, it's time."

Chase jumps up and starts running around the kitchen, racing his dinky car over the bottom cupboards.

"Oh, no, it looks like he got his second wind. I need to try to get him to bed now while I still can."

I stand with her as she chases after her son. "He's aptly named," I say, and it brings a smile to her pretty face, a smile that hits like a puck to the jaw. Goddammit, I'm the reason she no longer smiles like that.

"I'll take care of this pizza and lock up," I tell her. "You guys both need sleep."

"So do you."

I run my fingers through my hair. "Yeah, I do," I say. I need a lot of things, but no only do I not deserve them, I'm not about to share those thoughts with Fallon. My days of opening up and taking risks are over.

Every single noise, from the slightest creaks inside the house, to the cars passing by on the street below, has me jumping out of my skin and thinking about how many times I'd laid awake in bed waiting for Ethan's car to pull in after he'd been on the road. After hearing his vehicle in the driveway, I'd lay silently and wait for the stairs to creak under his footsteps. While I know he's never going to pull into the garage, never going to climb those stairs and crawl in with me, that still doesn't stop each noise from messing with my brain. Yeah, I'm definitely going to have to sell the place, sooner rather than later. The bed coils creak as I turn to face the wall. But it's short-lived and a second later I flip over to my other side, unable to settle myself.

Was it too soon to return?

Restless, I slide from the sheets and step into the hall to check on Chase, who thankfully is snuggled in tight and sleeping silently in his bed. Thank God for the resilience of children. My heart squeezes as I look at him, and I pray that Jamie can be the positive male influence he needs. Although after seeing the mental and physical state of Chase's uncle,

I'm not so sure. I don't want to put any pressure on him, or ask him to be something he can't, but deep in my heart I have a feeling a bond would be good for the both of them.

I fix the blankets around Chase and walk back into the hall. I make my way downstairs and boot up my laptop. I scroll through Facebook and Instagram. Oddly enough, I find myself doing a search for Jamie, although I quickly discover his accounts have been dormant for a little over a year now. So have mine. I do a quick search for real estate agents, and then another one on daycares. Since I'm up, I shoot an email off to human resources at Seattle General. I took an extended leave of absence, with the promise that my job would be waiting for me when I returned. After I fire off the email to Joyce, I close my computer. Hugging myself to ward off a chill I shouldn't be feeling in the warm house, I stand and wander through the place which, when it comes right down to it, truly is far too big for the two of us. I have no idea where we'll go from here, but I'd like to be in a community with small kids, near the hospital and good schools.

Stretching out my tired limbs as the wood floors creak from neglect, I notice that the clock on the kitchen wall has stopped. I almost laugh at the irony that time has stood still since I left. I make a note to change the battery tomorrow and head for the stairs. I'm on the third step when a loud noise outside reaches my ears. I jump, and grip the handrail, my heart thumping against my ribs.

Could Jamie be back?

Somehow doubting that, I sneak back into the kitchen and grab the baseball bat Jamie had set near the back patio door. I grip it, and flick the outside light back on. My hand goes to the lock, when I see a flash of someone or something running by.

"Oh, my," I shriek and jump back. Breathing hard, I hurry back up the stairs to my room and grab my phone. I grip it tight, and debate on calling Jamie. It's late and he's probably sleeping, but when I hear another bang, I dial his number.

"Hello," a groggy voice says on the other end. I've clearly woken him.

"Jamie. I'm sorry for waking you," I whisper.

"Fallon," he says, much more alert now. I hear his bed creak and can almost visualize him sitting on the edge of it. "What's wrong."

"I heard a noise. I was about to open my back door but then I saw a shadow. It wasn't you, right?" I ask, even though I know it wasn't. He's obviously at home in bed. Oh, shit. Another thought hits. What if he's not alone? What if he's with a girl, and I'm disturbing them?

"I'll be right there." Before I can protest, even though I'm not sure I want to, he continues with, "Go to Chase's room and lock the door. Don't hang up. I want you to stay on the phone with me."

I tiptoe into my son's room, shut and lock the door. I walk quietly to the window and peer through the curtains. I spot Jamie hurrying down the street.

"I see you."

Breathing hard into the phone, he glances up, and the streetlight falls over him. "You okay?"

"I am. I feel silly for calling. It was probably nothing."

"Or maybe it was something." He disappears from my sight, and through the phone I hear him walking along the pathway to the back yard.

"Anything?" I ask quietly.

"Not seeing anything, but that doesn't mean there wasn't someone snooping around. I want you to get an alarm system installed. I never did like you staying home alone without one. I talked to Ethan about it before, but he never got around to it."

He'd talked to Ethan about installing an alarm system?

"I don't plan on staying here too long, though."

"I'll make the arrangements tomorrow. I'm coming inside. That's me you hear at the back door."

"Okay."

I open Chase's door and close it quietly behind myself. I'm two feet from the stairs when Jamie reaches the top step, his hair a disheveled mess, his eyes tired and heavy from sleep. My gaze falls over his half naked, tattooed body.

Don't look.

Don't admire.

I look.

I admire.

Dammit.

My gaze slowly falls down, lingers over a chest that is rock hard, and stomach muscles that are defined and prominent. Holy, I've seen him shirtless before, but this...this...A strange, garbled moan I have no control over crawls out of my throat.

He comes to me, pulls my shaking body into his embrace, obviously mistaking my wounded sounds for fear. "It's okay. I'm here."

My hands go to his bare chest, and his heart pounds against my palm. "Where...why aren't you wearing a shirt?"

"I was asleep when you called. It was all I could do to get my pants on before running over here."

"Well it's a good thing you stopped to do that. I don't want you to get arrested for indecent exposure on my account." Although there is nothing indecent about his body. In fact, it's pretty decent, pretty decent indeed. The old Jamie would have made a joke about what I'd just said, but this Jamie is more subdued, and serious. Regardless, I shouldn't be looking at my brother-in-law sexually, shouldn't be taking this much pleasure in his embrace, either. But damn, he's so big and strong and comforting, and I need this, need his hugs, the warmth of his touch.

He inches back, and his gaze leaves mine, falls down the length of me and that's when I become fully aware of my attire. Same snug T-shirt he'd seen me in earlier, except no bra this time and only panties for bottoms. In the commotion, I forgot to dress, or even pull on a robe.

"Oh, sorry."

"What are you sorry for?" he asks, his voice an octave lower.

"I'm not wearing much."

He scrubs his chin. "I'm aware."

Oh, God, I can't even imagine what he thinks of all my plumpness. The man gravitates toward waif thin women. Sara was tiny, even pregnant there wasn't much to her—something Ethan used to comment on in a positive way. Personally, I think women should fill out during pregnancy. I certainly did. Only problem was, the weight was easy to put on, but not so easy to take off. I fold my arms across my big chest, as Ethan's words come back to me. *When are you going to lose the baby weight?*

Oh, how those mean words stung, but I don't like to think about that anymore. Ethan is gone, and I can't harbor negative thoughts. They're useless and destructive to my well-being.

"I'm going to spend the night," Jamie says, a statement, not a question.

I shake my head and my hair tickles my shoulders. "No, no. I've put you out enough already."

Ignoring my protest, he places big, heavy hands on my shoulders and turns me. "Go to bed, Fallon." He nudges me with his chest and a strange bolt of heat goes through me as his muscles press against my back. Okay, clearly I haven't been touched in far too long if a simple, innocent touch from my brother in law is messing with my mind and body.

When was the last time I'd been touched, anyway?

My thoughts go back and a disheartened groan catches in my throat. Ethan was so turned off by my curvy body that he'd barely touched me after Chase. Is it any wonder he...

I stop my thoughts.

Turning, I face my brother-in-law. "Thanks Jamie," I say. "I really appreciate you coming over."

His eyes latch onto mine, and his nostrils flare. What is going on with him? Was it something I said? He puts his hand over his head, grips the door frame hard as he stares at me with...hunger? Okay, I must be hallucinating. Jamie has never looked at me like that before. No man ever has, really. The drive here, the memories, the scare. Yeah, all those things must be messing with my perception of reality. It's the only logical explanation.

"Jamie?"

He tears his gaze from mine so fast, I'm sure he's given himself whiplash. "I'll grab one of the spare rooms," he informs me and walks away, leaving cold where there was once warmth.

With my door cracked so I can hear Chase, I hurry into my bed and draw the covers up to my neck, shaking for reasons I can't quite comprehend. I calm myself, and going perfectly quiet, I listen carefully to Jamie's heavy steps on the wood floor. The bedroom door closes with a click, and I strain to hear what's going on in the room next to me. Will he flop into bed in his jeans, or will he remove them and sleep naked between the sheets?

For a moment I visualize his removing his pants, his big, strong body, denting the mattress as he climbs in. Only I'm suddenly imagining he's not alone. No, it's me he's crawling in bed with, me he's looking at with hungry eyes, touching with needy hands, telling me I'm perfect...

A car speeds by outside and pulls me from my reverie.

What the hell am I doing? I suck in a fast breath to get myself together.

Don't go there, Fallon.

We're both very damaged people who can't go down that road. I'm sure he only told me I was perfect because he was being kind. Rolling to my back, I stare up at the ceiling, and take deep fueling breaths. I need sleep, and I need it now.

The next thing I know, I'm waking to the sound of pots banging in the kitchen. The noise startles me and I jackknife up in the bed. Where the hell am I? I glance around quickly, catalogue my surroundings, and relax slightly.

I'm back in my Seattle home. Jamie slept over, and it's probably him banging around downstairs. I glance at the clock and my jaw falls open when I see it's nearing noon.

Chase!

I fly from the bed and run across the hall. He's not there. Panic grips me, and I hurry downstairs, dash down the hall and practically skid to a halt when I find Chase sitting on the counter, stirring batter and chatting with Jamie. My heart jumps into my throat at the sight of the two.

"Jamie," I say breathlessly, and his head lifts. His eyes are heavy if not a bit sad as they fall from my face, to take in my near naked body. Dammit, I should have grabbed my robe, but I'd been so worried about my son. I fold my arms over my chest. "I woke up. Chase wasn't in his room. I...I never sleep that long."

"I'm sorry," he says quietly, in a calming manner. "Chase woke up and you were sleeping so soundly I didn't want to wake you. I didn't mean to scare you."

"No, it's okay. I appreciate you looking after him." I step up to my son, who is smiling as he stirs batter, and give him a big hug. "What are you making?" I ask him, and that's when I notice all the food on the counter.

"Pancakes," he informs me.

"Where did all this come from?" I ask Jamie.

"I put an order in." He shrugs like it's nothing but it's not. This was kind and thoughtful, and I'd been giving all my energy to raising Chase—had even been taking care of my mom after her fall a couple months back—that it's kind of nice not to shoulder the entire load by myself. "Had it delivered. No biggie."

I glance over the food. Fresh veggies, fish, chicken, fruit, and even the hummus I like. I shake my head, perplexed. "You remembered all my favorites?"

"I took a chance."

"And a few of your own," I say with a chuckle, when I see the big slabs of steak.

"Well, yeah. If you're going to call me in the middle of the night and wake me up, I should at least get a steak dinner out of it, don't you think?"

I laugh at that, really laugh and it feels good. Jesus, when was the last time I had a good belly laugh. Chase laughs with me, even though he has no idea what's funny, and so does Jamie. My God, it's good to see a glimpse of the witty, carefree man I once knew.

"Yes, the least," I say.

"Not to mention all the things I agreed to help you with to get this place ready for sale."

I nudge him with my hip and he stumbles. "I'm going to work you so hard this week, you're going to need the substance to keep going," I pause and point to the floor. "Otherwise you'll be down on your knees."

As soon as the words leave my mouth, I realize how sexual they sound. Or maybe they don't. Maybe just being around Jamie, dressed only in his jeans and barefoot, is messing with my dormant body—reminding me I'm a woman with needs. But I can't go down that road with him, and I'm sure he doesn't want to go down it with me, either.

It's wrong on so many levels, and besides that, he has numerous puck bunnies to play with. What would he want with me?

"I got a good start on today already. While you were sleeping, I called for pool repairs, and got hold of a company to come take a look at installing a security system. Both will be here Monday morning."

"Wow, all this before pancakes. Impressive."

His grin fades. "I don't want you to count on me. I'll just let you down," he says, and I frown at the level of seriousness in his voice. "But a security system...well, a security system never lets you down."

My heart skips a beat as I digest what he's saying. He might have been carefree before the accident, but I could always count on Jamie in the past. What makes him think he's not responsible or reliable now, or that he'll only let us down? I'm about to ask when Chase pulls the wooden spoon from the batter and puts it in his mouth.

"Chase, no," I say.

"Won't hurt him. It doesn't have raw eggs."

Still, I take the spoon, and help him from the counter. "How about you go grab your dinkies and did you see the car mat in your room? Why don't you bring it down, and play until the pancakes are ready," I say, and he darts off into the other room. At least the house is still baby-proof and I don't have to worry about him getting in to anything dangerous.

I walk over to the coffee pot and pour a generous amount into a huge mug. I add a splash of milk and moan as I drink. "Mmm, so good. Thanks, Jamie."

He gulps in a weird way. "You don't have to keep thanking me. I'm your brother-in-law and this is what Ethan would have wanted."

"Okay," I say. "Is there anything I can do to help?"

Jamie pours the batter into a hot pan, and it sizzles and

bubbles. "Nope, got it under control. Pancakes are my specialty."

"Only because it's the only thing you know how to cook."

"Hey, be nice. I make a mean mac and cheese."

"Oh, I remember your mac and cheese. The blackened kind that stuck to the bottom of the pot." Chuckling, I pull three plates from the cupboard and set them on the counter. "I only ate it to be nice."

"I'll show you nice," he says and picks up a wooden stick and slaps it against his palm.

"Don't you dare," I warn. I grab the tea towel, and start to spin it in my hand, ready to whack him in retaliation.

"Mommy," Chase says, breaking the playful moment as he drags a handful of dinky cars and his car mat into the kitchen. "Jamie said I could go swimming today."

"Not in that pool," I say, and cringe as I glance out the window to see the dirty green water.

"Mom and Dad were hoping we'd stop by this afternoon. I gave them a call. You mentioned visiting them, so I hope you don't mind. They'd love to see Chase and maybe he could take a swim in their pool. It's a hell of a heat wave we're having."

I set my coffee down and notice the small shake in my hand. "I'm not so sure why I'm nervous about seeing them."

Reading me so well, Jamie puts his hand on my arm. "They're not upset with you, Fallon. They understand you needed to be with your mother." He smiles but it's wounded and makes me think he didn't understand my need to escape. Then again, how could he? I used to turn to him for comfort, share things with him, but I couldn't in this situation—for reasons he can never know.

As his touch messes with me, heat rippling over my sex, I back away, and go about putting the groceries in the fridge. "I haven't been swimming in a long time." I laugh but it's not light and airy like I want. "None of my old suits will fit." I catch Jamie's eyes. "Baby weight," I say, feeling the need to explain again.

"Fallon—" he begins but I cut him off.

"I'll pay you for all these groceries."

He pauses for a moment, and follows my lead by saying, "Yeah, by cooking for me. I've been living off pizza and beer."

"And pancakes," I add.

He sticks his gut out and Chase laughs. "I won't fit into my hockey jersey at this rate."

I go still when my cell phone rings. I reach for it, and check the display, but it comes up as private. I slide my finger across the screen, and say hello. I glance up at Jamie when no one answers. "Hello," I say again.

"What's going on?" Jamie asks.

"Not sure." I shrug and hang up. "I guess whoever it was changed their mind."

I set my phone down as Jamie plates the pancakes and we all take a seat at the table, but as we do, a knot tightens in my throat. The normalcy of this, eating as a family around this big oaken table, is all too familiar.

I concentrate on my son as he reaches for the syrup. "Here, let me help," I say and pour a little on his plate. I hand the bottle to Jamie. Our fingers touch and my nipples pucker. I quickly pull back. What is wrong with me? I've touched him numerous times in the past, and never got all jittery like this before. Okay, maybe that's not entirely true. Maybe I did have a thing for the older Adams brother when I first met the two at a friend's party. But he went off to the NHL, and Ethan and I grew closer. After that, I stopped looking at Jamie as anything other than a friend, and eventually a brother-in-law.

Until now.

JAMIE

I had every intention of getting up with the sun and clearing out of the house before Fallon and Chase climbed from their beds. Yes, I agreed to help her empty the place of Ethan's things, but packing up his belongings is a solitary task and it's best if I don't spend too much time with this family, have them rely on me in any sort of way. I fucked their lives up enough as it is.

But when Chase woke up to empty cupboards, and Fallon was sound asleep, I couldn't just up and leave. I'm a lot of things, but I'm not a total prick. I just can't let anyone get too close and they deserve someone better than me in their life.

So why did I decide to buy steak for dinner, and take them to visit with Mom and Dad?

Probably because I missed Fallon and Chase so goddamn much, and I could see that she was nervous about visiting with my family—her in-laws—alone after taking off without so much as a word. But after today, I plan to make myself a little less accessible. They're both better off that way.

I glance over at Fallon, and take a peek at Chase in the rearview mirror as I make the short trek to my parents' house. When they downsized, they found a place close to me. I guess after losing one son, they wanted to be closer to the other.

"Mom and Dad are going to love seeing you two."

"I know," she says and gives me a smile. "They're good people, Jamie. They took me in like I was their own."

I laugh. "After raising two rambunctious sons, they really wanted a daughter."

"Now they have a rambunctious grandson."

"After Ethan and me, Chase will be a walk in the park for them," I say, and it brings a smile to her face.

"Oh," she says and turns to me. "I heard from Joyce at HR. My job is waiting for me, but I'm going to take a month to get the house on the market and find a new, smaller place near the hospital." She looks out the window, off in the distance. "I know it's not much time, but I need to occupy my mind."

"I can understand that."

"I know you can," she says and before I even realize what I'm doing, I reach across the seat and give her hand a squeeze. Our gazes meet for a second, and she tugs her hand back and puts it on her lap. "I have to get Chase into daycare, and find a nanny for my night shifts."

Shit, I'm home until practice starts up next month, but I can't make the offer to help out at nights. "I'm sure Mom would love to help out."

"I don't want to ask too much, or put anyone out," she says.

I take a left and pull into the driveway of Mom and Dad's new bungalow. Fallon sits up a bit straighter and glances at the house. "I knew they moved, but for some reason still had it in my head we'd be at their old place."

I unbuckle. "I'm still have a hard time getting used to it too."

We exit the car and I grab their bag as she helps Chase from his seat. "Mommy, I want to go swimming," he says.

"We're going to," she says. "But first you have to say hello to Grandma and Grandpa Adams."

The front door opens and Fallon goes a bit still when she sees my mom and dad standing there. Her gaze rakes over them, and in turn they take in their daughter-in-law and grandson. They don't come rushing out. No, instead they let Fallon and Chase come to them, like they're skittish animals who need to make the first move, and I can't help but think it's the best approach for all.

I cross around the car, put my hand on the small of her back, and slowly usher her forward. Mom's smile is wide, if not a bit wobbly, and that's when I notice the fine lines around her eyes are just a bit deeper today. My dad has his arm around Mom's shoulder, a stabilizing force, as his dark eyes brim with joy.

"Look who's here," I say, keeping things light.

"Fallon, Chase, it's so good to see you both," Mom says, and Fallon relaxes under my touch. Mom pulls her in for a hug when we reach the landing.

"Marion, it's good to be back."

The women hug and Dad and I exchange a look, one filled with pain and hope. I know they've been worried about me, but have kept mostly quiet as I work out my own demons. Do they think now that Fallon is back, it will somehow help me move forward? They always knew how close we used to be.

Fallon turns to give Dad a hug. "Barry," she says, her voice shaky as he pulls her in. After the hugs, she drops to her knees.

"Chase, can you say hello to Grandma and Grandpa."

"I want to swim," Chase says and we all chuckle.

"Chase, that is not polite. I asked you to say hello," Fallon says in a disciplinary tone of voice.

"Hello," Chase says, and my mom carefully reaches for his hand, but it's easy to see how excited she is, how much she wants to embrace him. But she's going slow. We all need to go slow.

"Now that we've gotten that out of the way, how about a swim?" Mom says.

Chase takes her hand, and as she leads him inside. We all follow. Fallon turns to me, gives me a smile that nearly stalls my heart.

"Thanks, Jamie," she says.

"Fallon—"

As everyone disappears around the corner, she puts her hand on my chest, and her touch goes right through, wraps around my heart in a way that's almost frightening. Jesus fuck, I've missed her.

"I know you don't like me thanking you, but I really, really appreciate you being here with me right now. It made this reunion that much easier."

I lean against the wall and swallow against the tightness in my throat. "That steak better have a pile of onions and mushrooms," I say working hard to keep everything I'm feeling hidden.

She laughs and it brings a smile to my face. "Still motivated by food, I see." She angles her head and looks me over. "Are you sure you're not part Labrador retriever? You do have the same dark eyes."

I cock my head. "Ah, was that a sideways insult?"

"No," she says, and whacks my stomach. I capture her hand, and hold it as I feign hurt. "I love dogs. I even thought about getting one for Chase."

Dad pokes his head around the corner. He's about to say

something until he sees how close we're standing. He disappears as quickly as he appeared.

I drop her hand like it's on fire—except I'm the one burning up inside—and inch back. "We'd better get outside before they wonder what we're doing."

She nods quickly, and I push off the wall. She follows me outside and I find Mom and Chase at the patio table eating watermelon as Chase fidgets in his seat. The kid doesn't like to sit still for long. I chuckle quietly. He's definitely a chip off the old block.

"Mommy, Mommy, look," Chase says holding up a slice of watermelon bigger than his head.

"Will you all be staying for lunch?" Mom asks hopefully, and I turn to Fallon, leaving this one in her hands.

"We would love to," she says and Mom gives her a big smile. This is good for Mom and for Fallon. They always liked each other, and I think a lot of healing might take place for both of them now that they're back in each other's lives. They both needed this. With Fallon's father gone, Dad will be a good father figure for Chase too. It's certainly not a role I can take on.

I drop down into a chair and reach for a piece of melon. Everything about this morning, from hanging out at the pool, to snacking on watermelon around the table, takes me back to my childhood with my brother, who would likely be doing cartwheels off the diving board right about now. That memory brings a smile to my face but also guts me at the same time. Fallon sits next to me, and I hand her a slice as Dad pulls a chair out across from me. He can't seem to stop smiling as he watches Chase.

"The place looks great," Fallon says to Mom. "I see you're still working your flower gardens. Mine are in desperate need of love."

"You know I can help with that." Fallon gives me a glance

like she's not sure how to break the news that she's moving. I'm about to come to her rescue when Mom says, "Barry is retiring soon, and we thought that old place was just too big for us." She rustles Chase's hair, which is little too long, like mine. "But we made sure to get a place with a spare room for you and Chase if you ever want to stay over."

Dad takes a sip of his lemonade, and fills three more glasses. "That's Marion's way of saying you guys are welcome here anytime and if you ever need a babysitter, don't hesitate to ask."

Fallon smiles, and brushes her honey blonde hair from her face. Her brow is damp from the hot morning son. "That's so nice. I'm sure Chase would love to spend time with you both."

"That' reminds me, Mom. Fallon is also looking to sell." Mom arches a brow, her eyes wide and worried.

"You're not leaving Seattle, are you?"

"No, just looking to downsize as well. I want to get a smaller place near a good school and close to the hospital. I'm going to be taking on some shifts. Just a few at first, but it's time." Both Mom and Dad go quiet as they nod in understanding.

"She's looking for a good realtor," I say. "You were happy with yours, right?"

"Oh, John Harrow is great. I have his card," she says. "I'll give him a call right now. See when he can stop by to assess your place."

"Thanks, Marion," Fallon says, as Mom picks up her cell phone and punches in the number.

"I need to get changed and cool off." I wipe my brow. "It's a scorcher."

Fallon stands and reaches her hand out to Chase. "Hey bud, you ready for that swim?" As mom talks to John Harrow, Chase takes another bite of his watermelon, and his face is all wet and dripping as he nods emphatically. Wiggling from his seat, he rushes to Fallon.

"It's all set," Mom says. "He'll stop by your place tomorrow."

"Tomorrow is Sunday."

"Not a problem for him. He's happy to help out."

"I really appreciate that," Fallon says. "What would I do without your help?" She turns to me. "Jamie has been great." She chuckles slightly. "He came running in the middle of the night when I called." She crinkles her nose. "I heard a noise and it frightened me. He stayed over, even cooked breakfast."

I clear my throat. "There have been a number of break-ins in the neighborhood."

Dad leans forward. "Perhaps you should stay with us, or with Jamie."

"I appreciate the offer, but Jamie made arrangements for an alarm system to be installed on Monday." She gives me a smile that pushes the air from my lungs and curls around my heart.

"That's our Jamie, always thinking three moves ahead," Dad says and gives me a nod.

"That's what makes him such a great hockey player," Fallon says as she captures Chase's hand. "Okay buddy, let's go get changed and get you in that pool." She goes still and looks around. "Wait, where should we change?" she asks as she reaches for her duffle bag.

"Come on," I give her a nudge with my shoulder. "I'll show you."

Dad turns to Mom and he leans in conspiratorially, whispering something in her ear as we head into the house. I really hope he doesn't think there's anything going on between Fallon and me. I can see how he could have misread the situation in the hall. I can't imagine he'd be too thrilled to think his oldest son moved in on his youngest son's wife a year after he died. I'm going to have to straighten him out about that.

Fallon follows me down the hall, and I point to one of the spare bedrooms. "You guys can take this room. Mom still has some of my old clothes in the other one," I say and jerk my thumb over my shoulder. "I'll meet you both at the pool."

As I walk to the room, my cell pings and I pull it from my back pocket to see a text from my buddy Cole. I guess word that Fallon was home got around fast. The guys locker room is worse than a hair salon full of grandmothers. We could out-gossip them any day.

Cole: Hey what's up.

Jamie: Just at Mom and Dad's with Fallon and Chase.

Cole: She home for good?

Jamie: Far as I know.

Cole: We're all about to vacation at Wautauga Beach, until practice starts up next month. Why don't you guys come? Chase would love it. He could play with Brandon. They'd have a blast. Zander, Sam and Daisy are flying in from Boston too. So are Quinn, Jonah and Scotty. Katee and Luke are there now.

Jamie: Not sure Fallon is up to that.

Cole: Offer is open. Rider can't make it, so his cottage is yours for however long you want.

My mind goes back to the cottages on Wautauga Beach, Port Orchard. It's a beautiful spot, with Mt. Rainier looming in the distance. A bunch of guys on the team all purchased property there years ago. Sara and I had planned on it, but it never happened. Cole is right, though. I'm sure Fallon and Chase would love it, and it would give Chase someone his own age to play with.

But while it would be nice for Chase to meet Cole and Nina's son Brandon, Zander's and Sam's daughter Daisy, and Quinn and Jonah's son Scotty, I'm not so sure I want to go to the cottage and play house. Yeah, not a good idea at all. I'm have no problems helping Fallon get her house ready for sale and running errands, but holed up with her in a cottage for a week or more, probably not a good idea. I shove the phone back into my pocket, make my way to the other spare room and dig a pair of my swimming shorts from the dresser. I dress quickly and notice the other bedroom door is still shut tightly. I give a soft knock when I hear Chase inside.

"Fallon, everything okay?"

A pause and then, "I don't think I'm going to swim."

"Why not."

Another pause and then, "I should have gone bathing suit shopping. I don't know what I was thinking grabbing this one."

"I'm sure it's fine. It's just us," I say. When the hell did she get so self-conscious? What happened to her over the last year or so? Did someone say something cruel to her. She never seemed like the type to worry about a few pounds, and fuck man, those pounds look good on her.

The door slowly inches open and she's holding her duffle bag in front of herself. "I don't think this is a good idea."

"Mommy, I want to swim."

"I know, bud. Maybe another day."

"I'll swim with him," I say before thinking it through. I'm not supposed to be bonding with these two.

She gives me an apologetic look. "No, Chase is my responsibility...I just." She glances down, but then the door swings open and Chase darts past us.

"Chase, wait," Fallon says and goes after him. I run to keep pace, and as soon as we get outside, Chase races to the pool.

"Chase," Fallon yells, and drops the bag. She grabs him before he jumps into the deep end. She goes down on one knee, and gives Chase a good hard lecture about the dangers of the pool. He pouts a little and she pulls him to her for a hug. It's easy to tell how much she loves her son.

"You need your water wings," she says. "Stay right here and don't move, okay?"

"I'll watch him," I say as she comes toward me, and holy mother fuck, it's all I can do not to let my gaze drop to take in her lush breasts and curvy hips. Drool is practically forming in the corners of my mouth. The bathing suit is tight on her, but goddamn, the way she fills it out, is messing with my ability to think straight. I shift slightly, heat coiling low and deep. No need for my folks to see my growing hard on. I sit down on the edge of the pool to cool myself down.

I pat the side. "Come sit, Chase. Put your feet in the water."

As he drops down next to me, both Mom and Dad ease themselves into the water. Fallon comes back, her chest heaving as she blows into the water wings. Unable to help myself my gaze drops, and her eyes dart to mine. She goes perfectly still for a moment, her eyes narrowing, her body shifting like she's trying to hide herself.

I tear my gaze away and slide into the water, needing the cold water to push down the heat rising up inside me. She's the last girl in the world I should be ogling. I turn to face my father, and from the look on his face, I'd gather he thinks so too.

5

FALLON

By the time we make it home from the in-laws, Chase is so exhausted from swimming and playing with his grandparents—who he totally adores—his eyes are dropping out of his head. I give him a light dinner of mac and cheese and tuck him into his bed. He instantly falls into a deep sleep and I take a moment to kiss his sweet face before heading back downstairs, our wet bathing suits in my hand.

I round the corner to the kitchen and find a restless Jamie opening and closing the back patio door, like he can't decide whether to stay or leave. Either that or the latch is broken and he's trying to fix it. Although I get the sense it's the former and not that latter. But after we had such a good day together, I can't quite understand why he's so anxious to leave. Hot date? That thought hits like a brick, and dammit, it's insane how much that sours my stomach.

For God's sake, get yourself together, Fallon.

He turns when he hears me entering the kitchen, and he's so handsome, his rock-solid presence so warm and comforting, it's all I can do to breathe. My gaze rakes over his face and in the dark depths of his eyes I catch hints of pain, uncertainty.

"I should go," he says, his voice a harsh whisper.

"Oh," I say, not wanting think too hard on the disappointment taking up residency in my gut, or how much I really and truly missed him...need him. He inches back, and as the quiet of the house closes in on me, a sense of loneliness weaves its way through my body. For the last year it was just Chase, Mom and me and I got used to the quiet. But now, after spending just a short amount of time with Jamie, I hate the idea of being in this big old place alone. It comes right down to the fact that I like spending time with him. I always have.

"Date?" I ask, not sure I want to hear the answer.

"No," he says quickly. "I just... It's late."

Trying to make light of the dark mood hovering like a foreboding rain cloud, I tease and say, "Not too late for a barbecue. You've mentioned those steaks a few times since you bought them." But as soon as the words leave my mouth, I berate myself for my selfishness. If he doesn't want to be here, he should go. I shouldn't be trying to entice him for my own needy reasons.

I shake out the bathing suits, wanting to drape them over a chair outside. Jamie takes in a fast breath as his gaze travels down the length of my sundress to the skimpy suit in my hand. A suit I must have looked ridiculous in, judging by the way Jamie tore his gaze away as my plump breasts spilled from the too-tiny top. Talk about bulging in all the wrong places. Did I repulse him in it, like I did his brother?

Dammit, Fallon, stop thinking about the negative things Ethan once said. The past is the past.

"Are you sure you're up to cooking?" he asks, once again avoiding my direct gaze. What the hell is going on with him?

"Of course." I step toward him and he stiffens. "Um, I just need to get by you to put these wet clothes outside."

His face relaxes, relief apparent in his eyes. "Oh, yeah, sure," he says and steps to the side.

Jeez, what did he think I was going to do? Jump him? If so, it's easy to tell he's pretty opposed to the idea. I open the door, and a blast of warm air hits me as I step out. My body brushes Jamie's as I go, and if I didn't know better, I'd think the quick intake of his breath had more to do with wanting me than not. I drape Chase's small suit over a chair and my bikini top slips from my hands. I bend to snatch it up, but when a tortured sound reaches my ears, I slowly turn to find Jamie staring at me, his nostrils flaring, his gaze narrowing like he's visually stripping me bare. He runs agitated hands through his too long hair and looks like a skittish animal about to flee.

"Jamie?"

"Yeah?" he grumbles.

"Why...why are you looking at me like that?"

He shakes his head, and steps outside, closing the distance between us with three long strides. "This suit," he says, running the damp material of my bikini top through his thumb and index finger. My body comes alive as I watch him, imagining him touching me with such intense focus.

"I know," I say quickly. "I looked ridiculous in it."

He laughs, a deep hoarse sound that goes through me and zeroes in on the needy spot between my legs. "Oh, is that what you think?"

"I noticed the way you looked at me in it earlier." I lower my head, self-conscious. "Ethan told me I should have ditched it if I could no longer fit into it. It's just that it's pretty, and I can't seem to bring myself to part with it...I guess I should have gone shopping."

His head rears back. "Wait, what the fuck did you just say to me?"

Oh damn!

"I'm sorry, Jamie," I say quickly and mentally scold myself. "I don't know why I said that about Ethan. He was your brother. I shouldn't have…It's just sometimes…"

"Sometimes he made you feel bad about yourself," he says, his voice a low rumbling growl that reverberates through me.

It's not a question, but I keep my head lowered and say, "Yeah, but none of that matters now."

He touches my chin, lifts it until our eyes meet. "It does matter, Fallon," he says between gritted teeth. He gives a slow shake of his head, his dark eyes latched on mine. "It matters a hell of a lot."

"No, it's in the past."

A moan that sounds like it was born of sexual frustration crawls out of his throat. "When I said you were perfect, I wasn't lying."

I shake my head. "You don't have to say things like that."

"You think I'm fucking lying?" he asks, his voice taking on a hard edge. Before I know what's happening, he pulls me to him, and my stomach connects with his erection. His very *big*, erection.

"Oh." My heart picks up pace, my body reacting to the strong, aroused man before me.

"Do you still think I'm lying, Fallon?" he asks, his voice infused with heat and need.

Jamie is aroused, because of me?

OMG, Jamie is aroused because of me!

"Um, no."

"You're beautiful, Fallon." He touches my face, runs a calloused hand over my cheek. "If you weren't my brother's wife, I'd…I'd take you to my bed and show you just how sexy you are, in a bikini or out of it."

I pause, take a long moment to digest his words, as his

dark brown eyes, full of lust and hunger roam my face. Something in his expression softens as his hand falls to mine. His warm knuckles brush mine and my entire body quakes with the need to feel a man's touch. But not just any man's touch. No, it's only Jamie's hands I want on me. It might have only ever been his.

"Out of it," I say quietly, not knowing what to do, say, or even think. He's my brother-in-law and the both of us are so goddamned damaged we're not thinking with any sort of clarity. But maybe what we're doing here is right, maybe...just once, we can find some sort of comfort in each other's arms.

Shaky hands go to my shoulders, and the air between us sizzles as he grips me tight. "What...what are you saying?"

"I'm not your brother's wife. Not anymore," I say as he looks at my mouth with hunger. A delicious shudder skitters through me at the heated look in his eyes. "I want you, Jamie. I want you to show me how sexy I am. Out of my bikini."

His throat makes a sound as he swallows, and after a low, tortured growl that floods my sex with heat, he says, "Fallon, I want you but you have to know I can't give you—"

I put my hands to his lips. "I don't want more, and I can't give more, either. Just this. Just tonight. Us."

His hand curls in the front of my sundress and he backs me up, pressing me to the wall like he did that first night he thought I was an intruder. His warm breath is on my face as his breathing becomes deeper, faster. "Tonight. Just tonight, Fallon. You and me. No one else."

"No one else," I say and I understand what he's asking. Our past, our hurts...they don't exist for the next few hours. No, tonight it's just two people, two best friends, in need of the other person's touch, for reasons neither of us are going to question.

His mouth lowers, and his lips land on mine. Soft at first,

an easy, careful exploration, but when I slide my arms around his back and pull him against me, wiggling and massaging his erection with my stomach, the kiss changes, becomes hungrier, deeper, a damaged man starved for so much more than physical touch.

I open for him, give myself over, wanting him to take charge, give me the freedom, the escape I need, the escape, I'm sure, I can only find with Jamie. As though reading my thoughts, he picks me up, holds me tight against his hard, protective body and for the first time in a long time, I feel wanted, feel like I no longer have to hide my curves.

"I've got you, Fallon," he says. "Tonight, you're mine. All mine. I'm going to take care of you," he says softly and I almost want to cry at the tenderness in his eyes. No man in the world has ever made me feel so protected, cherished.

"We're going to take care of each other," I whisper back as he takes me into the house, locks the door behind us and carries me upstairs. He brings me into the room he slept in last night, and I can't help but think it's a conscious decision. No memories of us come tomorrow in the bed I'm currently sleeping in. This is a one-night thing, and we both know it.

He closes the door quietly with his foot, then adjusts me in his arms. With the lights off, he carries me to his bed and positions me on the edge. I sink into the bedding, blink against the darkness, and work to make out his gorgeous frame as he stands back, far from my touch.

"Jamie," I say and reach for him, needing him in a way that is almost frightening.

I blink as the lamp on the night stand flicks on, and when my eyes adjust to the brightness, and I catch the intense way Jamie is staring at me, I suck in a fast breath, my pulse pounding at the base of my neck.

I perch on the edge of the bed, pretty sure I've never been

more anxious or needy about anything. When he doesn't make a move, doesn't do anything but stare at me a thread of nervousness ebbs its way through my brain, and as old insecurities creep back in, I begin to doubt everything, especially the part about me being perfect.

Has he changed his mind?

Not wanting him to read the worry on my face, or watch me run from the room if he's having second thoughts, I make a move to turn the light back out.

"Don't," he says so abruptly, so firmly my hand stops midair and my gaze flies to his. "I want to see you, Fallon. All of you. Every goddamn beautiful inch. I want to admire your full breasts, run my hands along your lush curves and bury my mouth between your legs until you're screaming my name and coming so hard nothing else in the world matters but what we're doing in this bed."

"I...I want that too," I say, barely able to hear as my heart pounds in my ears.

With that he tugs off his shirt and tosses it to the floor, gifting me an up close and personal view of his rock-hard body. My fingers itch and I'm practically salivating as I stare, memorizing every groove and valley to call on later, when I'm alone in bed. The man might have been letting a few things go this summer, but his fitness isn't one of them.

"Your turn," he says. "Shirt off."

I glance down at my sundress. "I don't have a T-shirt," I say and one corner of his mouth turns up in a playful grin.

"I know."

A chuckle bubbles in my throat, thrilled to see the playful Jamie back. "Fine then," I say and stand. I grip my dress, and hesitate for a brief moment before peeling it off. His eager eyes leave my hands and move to my face to assess me.

"You're beautiful, Fallon. I can't wait to get my mouth and hands on all your sweet curves. Trust me on that."

With his encouragement, a new kind of confidence bubbles up inside me. I pull my dress off and let it fall to the floor in a heap near his shirt. The groan that follows gives me a burst of confidence as I stand before him in nothing but my bra and panties. He rips into his jeans and kicks them off, and I take in his huge erection pressing insistently against his boxer shorts. Holy, the man is nothing short of perfection.

"Your turn," he says.

"I don't have pants," I say, playing along with this game as I study the tattoos on his body and consider their significance.

"I know," he says again, giving me that devilish grin that is turning me inside out.

"Fine then." I grip the thin elastic on my panties, toy with them for a minute and I'm about to pull them off when his voice stops me.

"Slow," he whispers, and my heart misses a beat. "Nice and slow, Fallon. I want to enjoy every second of this."

I gulp. Good God, I've never done a strip-tease before, but I'm sensing that's exactly what he wants from me, and I can't help but want to give it to him. Who knew that behind closed doors Jamie would be a dirty-talking, take charge kind of guy. I almost want to stand on the roof and scream hallelujah. I wiggle my hips and his tortured moan fuels the hunger in me.

"Like this?" I ask and move my hips, rotate them in a way he clearly finds sexy, judging by the harsh breathing sounds he's making.

"Just like that," he says softly, and pulls his cock from his boxer shorts. He strokes himself and I can't believe what I'm seeing. The man has no shame and I absolutely love it.

"Turn around," he says, his voice a soft command that excites me on even more. As my sex moistens in anticipation, he continues with, "Legs together, knees locked, and bend forward to remove your panties."

A thrill races through me when I get what he's after. I turn, and keeping my legs together, and knees locked, I slide my panties down my thighs, giving him a view of my very curvy backside. Never in my life would I have had the guts to do something like this, even when I was thin. But something about this man, something about the way he's gazing at my body—like he wants to worship every inch of me—heats me in a way I've never been heated, and kicks any lingering self-doubt out the door.

"Yeah, that's it. That's so fucking it," he growls. "So hot, Fallon. So hot I might just come in my hand." A little yelping sound rises in my throat as I discard the panties. "Now turn around and show me that pretty cunt of yours. I want your legs spread wide for me."

I turn on wobbly knees and face him. No man has ever talked to me the way he is right now. But damned if I don't need it—love it. It makes me more eager to hand myself over to him, let him do whatever he wants to my quivering body. His gaze drops to take in my sex and I widen my legs without hesitation, bare myself to him. My sex is hot and wet, aching for his touch. His eyes jerk to mine, and he brushes his tongue over his bottom lip.

"I can't wait to get my mouth on you," he whispers his voice rough with urgency.

"What are you waiting for?" I say, bolder than I ever have been in my entire life.

He tears off his boxers and steps up to me. Sliding one hand around my waist, he none so gently tugs me firmly against him. Our bodies crash. Burn against each other. His other hand opens my bra with an expertise I don't want to think about. He frees my full breasts, and his gaze drops to take in my nakedness as my lacy bra sails to the floor.

"Fucking gorgeous," he says and cups both breasts, kneading and squeezing so hard my sex clenches with pleasure. His thumbs brush my nipples and they harden even more. I've never come from nipple stimulating before, but I'm close, so close it's insane. "These are all mine tonight."

"Yes," I say and he dips his head, takes one marbled nipple into his mouth and sucks so hard I throw my head back and shamelessly cry out his name.

"Yeah, I like when you do that," he says, and treats the other nipple to the same stimulation. I grip his shoulder and hang on as he licks, nips and sucks and takes his fill of me. My fingers itch to touch him in return, so I slide a hand between our bodies and grip his throbbing cock. He's so damn thick I can barely fist him and I quiver all over at the thoughts of him filling me.

"Jesus, that feels good," he murmurs, his mouth going to my neck. He kisses the sensitive hollow spot as I stroke the length of him. With a little nudge I fall backward onto the bed, and land on the mattress. My heavy breasts bounce from the movement and he groans in pleasure.

"So sexy," he says and drops to his knees. He grips my thighs, and widens me until my sex is on full display. He finds my mouth, kisses me deeply as he runs his fingers along my legs, squeezing my thighs. "Soft and plush and all mine," he says as he breaks the kiss.

He takes my hands which are braced at my sides and places them on my breasts. He keeps his hands on mine, and squeezes, forcing me to massage myself. "Do you touch yourself like this when you're alone?" he asks.

"Yes," I murmur, and he squeezes my tits together, his growl of approval ripping through me.

He pulls his hands away, and I continue to rub myself. "I like watching you do this."

"I like watching you too," I admit.

He grins. "I can't wait to fuck these," he says. "But first I've been dying to get my mouth here." One hand slides between my legs, circles my engorged clit, teasing relentlessly until I'm squirming on the bed. "What's the matter, Fallon?" he asks, a playful edge in his voice. "You need something."

"You know I do," I cry out.

"What is it you need, babe? Tell me, I'll give it to you. Anything you want. I'll take care of you. Tonight, anything you want, you get."

"I want your mouth on me. I want your fingers inside me. Please..." Lost in euphoria, I lift my hips, my entire body begging, clamoring for so much more from this man.

He slides one thick finger into me and I throw my head back and groan. "This what you need?"

"Yes," I cry out.

He wiggles his finger inside me, and my body ripples. "You like that?"

"Oh, yes," I say and move my hips. He draws his finger out, and slides it back in again. Sensations rocket through me, and draw me deeper and deeper into a place where only pleasure exists.

"I want your cum all over my fingers," he says. "I want you all nice and hot and slick when I put my cock in you."

Holy God, who is this man?

"Yes, Jamie," I say on a breathless whisper. "It's been so long. Too long. Years," I murmur without thinking as I toss my head from side to side, and squeeze my full, aching breasts. His finger goes still high inside me and that's when my one last working brain cell sparks to life, and warns that I shouldn't have revealed something so personal. Cripes, it's just that I'm not thinking straight. Apparently, Jamie's touch does that to me.

Get it together, Fallon.

I move my hips, letting him know what I want, and he

starts to finger fuck me again, sliding another one in for a snug fit. "That is so good," I cry out without shame.

He leans in, and licks my clit, and his growl thrills me. "So fucking sweet, Fallon. If I didn't need my cock in you, I'd spend the night feasting on your sweet cunt." He pulls his fingers from my sex and tongues me as his thumb presses against my swollen cleft. I can't believe how close I am to coming, and I'm thinking it has more to do with Jamie's deft fingers and tongue rather than how long it's been since I've been with a man.

He touches the sensitive bundle of nerves inside me and my breath stalls. Every ounce of pleasure centers on my core and my muscles start clenching, pulsing, squeezing his finger as my hot release bursts over me.

"Oh, my... Yes, Jamie," I cry out.

"That's it. Come for me, baby." He laps at me and continues to fuck me with his fingers as I come and come and come some more. Years of pent up tension drain from my body with my powerful release and drip down Jamie's fingers and hand. "Yeah, just like that," he murmurs as he strokes me to prolong the pleasure.

I can't breathe let alone swallow when my body finally stops spasming. I blink but can't see, I gulp air but can't fill my lungs as Jamie slowly pulls his fingers out. He presses his forehead to mine, and breathes with me until the room comes back into view and my world stops spinning.

"You good?" he asks.

As I nod, he inches back and brings his fingers to his mouth. He licks himself clean and when he meets my gaze, he's wearing my moisture all over his face. It's the sexiest thing I've ever seen.

"I...don't think I've ever come like that before," I admit. Aren't I one for spilling all my secrets tonight.

A perplexed look comes over his face, then his eyes soften and he says, "You think you're done?"

I swallow against a dry throat. "I've never come more than once," I say.

He chuckles. "That's about to change," he says, not in a cocky way, but in a confident way.

"I don't think—"

"That's right. I don't want you to think." He stands, and his cock is right there, right in front of my mouth, pre-come dripping from his crown. If I wanted him in my mouth— wanted to wet my parched throat—all I'd have to do is part my lips. "When my cock is inside you, you don't think. You just feel."

"I don't want to think, Jamie." Needing to taste him, I widen my lips, lean forward and take him into my mouth until he hits the back of my throat. "Holy fuck, Fallon," he cries out and grips my hair.

I glance up at him with a mouthful of his fat cock, and take in the shock and heat in his dark eyes. "What," I say, sliding him from my lips. "You don't like?" I stroke the long length of him, and cup and massage his balls as they draw tight.

"Oh, I like. I like a lot." His grip on my hair tightens as I take him in again, running my tongue over his long length, and licking his bulging veins as they fill with heated blood.

I soften my tongue, run it over his crown and murmur, "I like it too." Those words seem to do something to him, something fierce and carnal. His hips power forward, and I relax my throat as he slides into it. Never in my life have I taken a man so deeply before, but with him, I can't get enough. I want him all. I want everything.

He tugs on my hair, but I want more, I want him to come in my mouth, but he has other ideas. I moan in protest when he inches out of my mouth, but that moan turns to a whimper of pleasure when I see the fire in his eyes.

He grips my arms, lifts me to my feet and plants a kiss onto my mouth. "I need to fuck you," he growls, and slides a hand between my legs. He strokes my hot sex, inserts a finger. "I think you need that too."

"I need this," I say and wrap my hand around his throbbing cock.

He picks me up, climbs onto the bed and walks on his knees to center me on the mattress. Widening my legs, he climbs in between them, and falls over me, taking my hard nipple into his mouth. "I know I need to spend more time here, but it will have to wait. Right now, I need inside your sweet pussy." He plunges a finger into me, and I swear I nearly come again.

Going back on his heels, he grips his cock, strokes twice and lets his gaze fall from my face to my legs and back again. Goosebumps break out on my skin, even though he hasn't even touched me, but his gaze strokes over my flesh like a caress. No man has ever looked at me with such worship in his eyes. I don't know whether to laugh or cry. "I'm going to make this so good for you, you're going to feel the effects a week from now. I promise you that," he murmurs.

"Please, Jamie."

He leans over me, and positions his crown at my center. His nostrils flare, and my entire body quakes, so damn eager for him to fill me. But then he clenches his jaw, the muscles rippling in the lamplight and my heart goes into my throat. Please tell me he's not having second thoughts. I'm about to squirm out from beneath him, but he pins me with his body weight.

"Condom," he murmurs. "I don't have a fucking condom."

"Oh, I thought…"

His eyes narrow on mine. "Thought what?" he asks.

"I thought...I thought you'd changed your mind," I say.

He stares at me for a long moment, then shakes his head. "Fuck, Fallon. You are the hottest woman I know. The sexiest. I am the luckiest guy on the planet right now."

I study the heat in his eyes, the way black pupils bleed into the brown. There is nothing in his expression to suggest he's lying, and that thrills me to the core. Heat sparks through me, a new kind of need zinging through my body.

"I'm on the pill, and I'm clean. I haven't been with anyone in a long time."

"I've been with women, Fallon. But I always use a condom. Always."

"Oh, okay," I say, and swallowing down the disappointment rising up in my throat, I begin to squirm out again.

He presses down on me. "No, you don't understand. I want you. Condom or not. I want you and what I meant was, I'm clean. I've never had sex without a condom before. Not even with..."

He lets his words fall off, but he doesn't need to finish the sentence for me to understand. "Fuck me, Jamie. Put your cock in me. It's what I want."

With a nod, he presses his mouth to mine, and powers into me. Air leaves my lungs in a whoosh as he spreads me wide, fills me in a way I've never been filled before. He stills high inside me, giving me a second to catch up.

"You good?" he asks after a long moment.

"Better than good," I answer and move my hips. He growls into the hollow of my throat.

"I'm so fucking close already," he murmurs, and inches out, only to slide back in again. I put my legs around him and run my hands through his damp hair as we fuck, both taking and giving what we need to sate the physical ache inside us.

I instinctively match each thrust as our bodies join as one.

It's as though they were always made for each other. He thickens more inside me, and I groan.

"You feel so good," I cry out, and run my nails along his back. His muscles bunch and clench, and it's strange how I like the idea of marking him, like the idea of seeing my scratches on his back come tomorrow.

"Maybe I am having second thoughts," he whispers into my throat. "Maybe I want to keep on fucking you, Fallon."

"Jamie," I say as his thrust become harder faster. He shoves a hand between our bodies and presses down on my clit. "I...I..." I swallow, as my mind shuts down and pleasure races through me, centers between my legs.

"Let go, Fallon. Come all over my cock."

I briefly pinch my eyes shut as sensations roar through me, grip my sex hard, and a second later, I'm vibrating all over his beautiful cock as it pistons into me. A soft moan of pleasure rises from my throat as my hot juice tickles my inner thighs and coats his cock.

"Holy fuck, that's hot," he murmurs, and throws his head back, his cock powering into me with blunt, hard strokes that are for him now. He pumps, and his eyes shut as he chases his own orgasm. I stop spasming, but squeeze my sex muscles and his body tightens. His grunts, and his face contorts and I'm sure I've never seen him look more beautiful.

"I feel you," I cry out as he stills high inside me and spills his seed into my body.

"Fallon," he growls as his cock continues to pulse. "Jesus, Fallon."

I hold him tight, our hot wet skin clinging as he falls on top of me, still buried deep in my body. His breathing is harsh against my neck, and I rake my hands through his hair. We stay that way until he grows flaccid and pulls out. He rolls, pulling me with him, and I rest my head against his chest, taking pleasure and comfort in his strong heartbeat. My lids feel heavy, but I don't want to sleep. No, I want to stay awake and enjoy every second of this for as long as I can.

His breathing changes, grows more shallow and when I think he's fast asleep, I speak into the silence of the room.

"Thanks, Jamie."

6

JAMIE

"*Thanks, Jamie.*"

I was almost asleep when those sweet words, spoken so softly and so sincerely pull me from my slumber and have me wanting to bury myself in her again and again. I lift my head and glance at the beautiful woman falling asleep on my chest. As I gaze at her, one thing hits. I should go. I should run as far away as possible. I don't deserve her. I don't deserve to be in her bed, and more importantly I don't deserve to be thanked. Not after everything that had happened. She lost Ethan because of me.

That thought gives me pause. My younger brother was wild and reckless and at times when we were growing up, he could be a real selfish prick. But he was my younger brother, and I loved him. Still, no man should ever make a woman feel bad about herself. A spike of anger prowls through my blood and burns me from the inside out. Then another thought hits. In the heat of the moment, Fallon said she hadn't been touched in years. Were they no longer intimate, no longer having sex?

Speaking of sex, I told her I wanted more.

Not my wisest move, but in the heat of the moment, I knew one night was never going to be enough, not when it came to Fallon. Sweet Fallon, who, if I'm being honest, I've wanted for far too long now. But somehow, some way, I'm going to have to make last night enough. She deserves better than me in her bed.

Fallon makes a soft, content whimpering sound in her sleep, and her arm slides across my body, pinning me down. If I move now, I'll wake her, and if she looks at me with those soft, sated eyes, I'll never be able to make my escape. I have no choice but to stay put until she moves to her own side of the bed.

With that last thought, I try to quiet my mind, catch a few minutes of sleep before I sneak out under the cover of darkness. The next thing I know, the sound of Chase running in the hall wakes me. I turn and find a wide-eyed Fallon looking at me.

"Oh, no," she says.

"Shit, I fell asleep," I say. "I didn't mean to."

"Not your fault, Jamie. I fell asleep too." She slides off her pillow, and goes deeper under the covers. "He shouldn't see us like this."

The bedroom door flings open, and I shift so Chase can't see his mother's outline beneath the sheets. Chase stands at the doorway and blinks.

"Daddy?" he asks, his eyes big and confused at seeing me in the bed, and my heart jumps into my throat.

"No, it's me, bud," I say, my voice a bit shaky. "Uncle Jamie."

He rubs his sleepy eyes, and my throat tightens as he frowns. "Where's Mommy?"

"How about some pancakes?" I say and change the subject.

"I want to stir."

"Of course. You're the best stirrer I know. Why don't you run into your room and grab your dinky cars. I'll be right there." He makes a motor sound, and flies down the hall. That gives me enough time to pull on my pants and shirt.

"I'll be down in a few minutes," Fallon whispers from under the blankets.

"Take your time," I say. "I'll keep him busy."

"Thanks, Jamie."

This time I don't bother saying anything. Instead, I dart into the hall, and help Chase carry a plastic bucket full of dinky cars downstairs.

"Where's Mommy?" he asks again as he looks around the kitchen.

"She's coming down. She was just busy," I say and the explanation seems to be good enough for him. I pick Chase up, set him on the counter and dig in the cupboard for the pancake mix. "Okay, buddy. Ready to make your mommy some breakfast?" I ask.

He nods and I pour the batter and milk into a bowl. I hand him a fork, and as he stirs, I go about getting the coffee ready. No doubt after such a frightful awakening, Fallon will need a cup or two when she comes down. I turn at the sound of her rushed footsteps in the hall.

"There you are," she says coming into the kitchen, and Chase's face lights up when he sees her. Heck, so does mine. Jesus, she's incredible. Need wells up inside me as I take a moment to admire her flushed face, a bit rubbed and red from my stubble. Barely able to catch my breath, I gaze at the long column of her neck, where her pulse raced against my tongue last night. Her hair is a tumbled mess, and her full breasts press hard against her too snug AC/DC T-shirt that I hadn't seen her wear in years. My gaze falls to take in frayed shorts that showcase her curvy hips. I've never seen her more beautiful. Decadent.

"Mommy, I'm making pancakes again," Chase says.

She gives me a grateful smile. "I can see that. You're such a great help." She steps up to him, gives him a hug and a kiss, and for a moment I stand there, wishing I was the recipient of her attention.

"Morning," she says to me quietly, her knuckles brushing against my arm as she reaches into the cupboard to grab two mugs.

"Coffee will be ready shortly," I say and she smiles.

"Mmm," she moans, and stretches out her limbs. "A girl could get used to this."

Her words race through me, remind me I'm not supposed to be here this morning. Fuck man, I shouldn't even have slept with her last night. We obviously need to talk, and I need to reinforce that last night was a one-night thing, despite what I said.

Maybe I want to keep on fucking you, Fallon.

Christ, what a dumb-ass thing to say. I mean, I can't deny that it's true—I want her between the sheets again—but I never should have spoken the worlds out loud. When it comes right down to it, we both agreed to one night, and I'm sure Fallon wants that too, although judging by the way she keeps brushing up against me, maybe I'm wrong about that.

"You good?" I ask quietly.

Dark lashes fall slowly over her blue, sated eyes, and I have to say, the morning after a round of sex is a good look on her.

"Yeah, you?"

I lower my voice. "Yeah, but I think we need to talk."

Her eyes widen, but she quickly pulls herself together and nods. "Yeah, sure."

Just then her cell phone rings, and she frowns. "Who could that be?" She reaches for her phone, and slides her finger across the screen. I grab the milk, pour a splash into our mugs, and she puts her hand over the phone and mouths the word, "Realtor."

I nod, and go about making our coffee. I hand her a cup and she gives me a grateful smile.

"How's that batter, buddy?" I ask Chase.

"I want to go swimming," he says, and it takes me back to my phone call with Cole. I have no doubt Chase would love to spend time at the beach with kids his own age.

"Looks like he's coming by shortly," Fallon says as she slides her finger across the screen to end the call.

I glance at the clock. "It's kind of early, isn't it?"

"Early bird gets the worm," she says, and Chase groans.

"I don't like worms, Mommy."

"Have you ever been fishing, Chase?"

He shakes his head no, and once again I think of the cottage. Before I can stop myself, I blurt out, "Cole texted me yesterday. All the guys are going to the beach for the next couple weeks. There will be a couple kids there as well."

"Are you going?" she asks.

"I don't know. Just putting it out there. I thought Chase—"

"Oh, you're asking if we want to go."

"Yeah, I guess."

She glances at me over the rim of her mug. "I'm not sure that's a good idea. I have so much to do to get this place ready. But you should go, be with the guys."

"We'll see." Why the hell am I so disappointed when I thought it was a bad idea anyway?

Chase squirms on the counter. "I'm hungry."

"Okay, little man," I say. "Let's get this show on the road."

I grab a pan, heat it and pour the batter in. Soon enough we're all sitting around the table, and Chase points to the ink on my arms.

"What is that?" he asks and for a brief second I fear he's pointing to the scratch marks Fallon left on my body.

I glance down. "What's what?"

"That," he says and points to the tattoo of the Stanley Cup.

"This is because our hockey team won a few years back. It's called the Stanley Cup." I take a bite of food and wash it down with a swig of coffee. "Have you ever played hockey, Chase?"

He shakes his head no, and it crushes me. Ethan had about as much interest in hockey as I do in ballet. But what's really bothering me is Chase is going to grow up without a strong male influence and the fact that he's going to miss out on so much. I don't want to get involved. Fuck knows I'd only end up letting them down, but maybe I could take him to the rink, let him try it, at least once.

I cast Fallon a quick look. "It might not hurt for him to go to the rink."

She smiles at me. "I'd be okay with you taking him."

"If he likes it, you could sign him up in the fall."

"I could do that," she says, grinning at me like the cat that ate the canary. What is that all about?

"More coffee?" I ask.

"Sure."

I grab her cup and fill her up. We make small talk as we finish breakfast, and once the dishes are cleared, and Chase is off playing with his toys, I grip her hand, tug her to me.

"Last night," I begin, her body so close to mine it's all I can do to keep a coherent thought. "It was—"

"Amazing."

I chuckle. "Yeah, that it was, but I said things I probably shouldn't have."

"You aren't the only one." She bites her lip and glances down.

That gives me pause. I don't want to delve into the personal here, but I suspect it's a bit too late for that. "Can I ask you a question? If you don't want to answer, you don't have to."

Nodding, she gathers her hair in her hand, pulls an elastic from her wrist and ties it up, exposing the long column of her neck. My mind goes back to last night, to the way I buried my face in that hollow of her throat as I came inside her. I fight down a growl of longing, and work to pull myself together.

"Were you and Ethan having problems?" Her entire body goes stiff, and it instantly answers my question. "That's what I thought," I say quickly.

Her lashes flash rapidly over blue eyes. "I never should have said anything about Ethan, Jamie. I'm sorry. In the moment, I—"

"It's okay. It's me, Fallon," I say softly. "We used to always talk, remember."

"I remember," she says so quietly I have to strain to hear it. "The truth is, Jamie, we *were* having problems. He was away from home more and more, and I tried to lose the weight, but it wasn't easy and I think that could be one of the reasons why..." She lets her words fall off and turns from me, but not before I catch the pain in her eyes. What is she's not telling me?

"Fallon?" She opens her mouth, like she wants to say more, but then closes it again. "I loved my brother," I state.

"You were good to him and he was a good father when he was home," she says quickly, and it doesn't go unnoticed that she left out that he was a good husband, and that he in turn was a good brother to me. I'd been too busy with hockey and getting engaged, and Sara's pregnancy to realize their marriage was failing. Once again, I let Fallon down.

"I'll always love him, but that doesn't mean I always liked

or agreed with everything he did or said." I take her hand in mine, turn her toward me. "There is no excuse for what he said to you, or how he treated you."

Tears pool in her eyes. "Jamie, I can't..."

"Okay, I just want you to know that." I scrub my face. "Also, last night, being with you. Jesus, Fallon." I exhale slowly and shake my head. "But I don't think we should do that again."

"I understand," she says. "It was a one-time thing. I think we just both really needed each other and I don't want it to come between what we have."

I give her hand a squeeze. "It won't."

"Promise," she says.

"I promise."

"Thanks Jamie." A growl rises in my throat but it's drowned out by the doorbell. "That was fast," she says, and I follow her to the door. She swings it open, and on the stoop, a middle-aged man dressed in a button-down shirt and dark grey dress pants gives her a big toothy smile.

"Fallon?"

"Yes."

"John Harrow," he says and holds his hand out for a shake. "So nice to meet you. Marion said you were looking for a realtor."

"That's right and I appreciate you coming so quickly."

"My pleasure," he says and after Fallon invites him inside, his gaze lands on me and he nearly fumbles.

'You're...you're..."

Fallon laughs. "John, this is Jamie Adams. But I suspect you already know that."

"Nice to meet you, John," I say and shake his hand.

"I'm a big fan," he gushes, and I grin at him. "I never got to meet you when I sold your Mom and Dad's place, but I watched every game you played."

"Thanks. Always nice to meet a fan." Chase comes running into the room, making noises and pretending he's driving a race car. I scoop him up. "This little guy is Chase, and we'll get out of your way so you can have a look around."

I open the closet door, where Ethan kept his sports equipment, and grab two ball gloves and a ball. "Come on, bud. Let's go out back and play catch."

The warm mid-morning sun beats down on the backyard as I fit my hand into the glove and hand Chase the smaller one, which is still too big for his little hand. We toss the ball back and forth for a bit until Chase grows bored.

"I want to go swimming," he says and eyes the dirty green pool.

"You know what." I toss the ball up into the air and catch it in the glove. "The pool is going to be cleaned tomorrow, so maybe we'll be able to get in it afterward."

"I want to go now," he pouts and I toss him the ball.

I glance up as Fallon and John step outside to examine the back yard. Chase takes the ball and tosses it up in the air—mimicking me—and tries desperately to catch it in his too-big glove. As I watch him the full weight of my influence over him hits me. Goddammit, I can't take that on. What if I fuck it up? I've fucked up enough as it is.

"Pool cleaners are coming tomorrow," Fallon explains. "And I know just the person to help with the gardening." She gives me a smile, and I know Mom would love that.

"Well, other than clearing out a bit of the clutter, and cleaning up back here, I think the place is in great shape. We can get it on the market right away."

Fallon's smile is wobbly and I get that a part of her is happy to sell, but there's also a part that is reluctant. I go back to playing with Chase as she talks to John about searching out smaller houses near the hospital as they head inside.

A few minutes later she sticks her head back out the door. "That went better than I thought. No staging or painting needed."

"The house is only five years old, plus you haven't been here this last..." I let my words fall off as her eyes grow watery. "Fallon," I say and step up to her. "If it's going on the market right away, I should get to work on clearing the closets. Do you want to take some time today to go through things?" I ask.

She nods. "I can do that today."

"Chase is asking if he can go swimming. Why don't I drop him with Mom and Dad? That will give you time to yourself, and I'll come back and take care of the things you want to throw out or donate."

Her gaze leaves mine and falls over her rambunctious son. "I don't know. He just got reacquainted with them yesterday. Is it too much to ask them, and will he be okay alone without me?"

I grin. "Watch this." I turn to Chase. "Hey buddy, you want to go swimming with Grandma and Grandpa?"

"I do. I do. I do," he says and starts running in a circle. Fallon laughs and it brings a smile to my face.

"Chase, come here," she says.

He runs over and she drops to her knees. "Uncle Jamie is going to take you and I'm going to stay here because I have some things do to. Is that okay?"

"Okay, Mommy," he says.

Fallon rolls her eyes at me. "Wow, I feel so important." She stands. "Okay, let's get your bag packed." She takes his hand. "You don't think they'll mind?"

"Positive. I'll call now." I grab my phone and call as Fallon gets Chase ready. By the time she comes back downstairs, Chase now out of his pajamas, I say, "They're thrilled. They asked if they could keep him for dinner as well."

"You want to have dinner with Grandma and Grandpa, Chase?" Fallon asks.

"I want watermelon," he yells.

I snort. "I take that as a yes."

Fallon hands me her keys. "Take my SUV. It has the car seat in the back." Fallon follows us outside, and buckles Chase in. I shut the door and turn to her, see the strain in her eyes. A lump clogs my throat and there isn't a thing I can do to swallow it down.

"You going to be okay?" I ask, and resist the urge to pull her in for a hug, tell her everything is going to be okay. Because it's not. Nothing will ever be okay for her again. Last night, for a short time we were able to lose ourselves in each other, forget about life for a while, but now, under the stark light of reality, the world once again weighs heavy on her.

Because of me.

"As good as can be expected," she answers with a forced smile.

"I won't be long. I'll get Chase settled and be back." Before I open the driver's side door, I ask, "Starbucks, salted caramel latte?"

Her eyes practically roll back in her head and it's almost the same look she gave me when she was coming in my arms. "You remember."

"Yeah, I remember," I say. "Okay, see you shortly." I climb into the driver's seat and start the vehicle.

As I back out, Chase says, "I want to hear the alligator song."

"No idea what that is, bud," I say as I adjust the rearview mirror and glance at him.

"Press that button." He points at the console and I scan it until I figure out what he's pointing at. I press the DVD play button, and the next thing I know some god-awful song blares through the speakers. Chase starts singing along and I cringe. What the ever-loving fuck am I listening too? Behind me, Chase starts chomping his hands to the beat and I wish I had ear plugs because now I'm going to have an earworm for the rest of the day. Fuck man, how can Fallon listen to this?

I drive through the light morning traffic and Chase is practically jumping in his seat when I pull up to Mom and Dad's place. They come out the door when they see us. I exit the vehicle.

"Thanks guys," I say. "I'm helping Fallon get the house ready today, so watching Chase is a big help."

Mom comes from the steps and Chase instantly goes to her. She scoops him up for a hug. "You go ahead. He's in good hands."

"Don't I even get a hello or a hug?" I say, and laugh when Mom shoos me away.

My father snorts. "Take all the time you need, son," he says, and they all disappear inside.

"Don't forget his water wings," I call out.

"It's not our first rodeo," Dad calls back to me and I just shake my head. No, I suppose it's not and Ethan and I were the rodeo clowns who'd given them most of their gray hair.

I head to Starbucks and drive back to Fallon's, hoping I gave her enough time to go through Ethan's things. My heart squeezes. What she's doing can't be easy. I ease into the driveway, grab her latte, and walk into the house to find it quiet.

"Fallon," I call out.

"Up here," she says, and I follow her voice and find her in her room sitting on her bed, going through old photo albums. I hand her the latte.

"Thanks, Jamie," she says, putting it on the nightstand and patting the mattress beside her. I sit next to her and glance at the pictures, but it's the tears in her eyes that are holding my attention. I slide my hand around her back and she leans into me.

"You okay?" I ask quietly.

"I am," she assures me, and I hug her tighter. "Remember this?" she says, her words a half laugh, half cry.

I glance at the picture of us in Mom and Dad's pool from a years ago, before Chase was born, and I made the NHL. Fallon is on my shoulders, and her friend Maria is on Ethan's, and the girls are trying to knock each other off using water noodles like they're jousting lances. I laugh and shake my head.

"Seems like that was just yesterday."

"We won," she says, with a small smile as she gazes at the picture like she's a million miles away.

I nudge her. "That's because we were a good team."

"Yeah, we were," she says, an almost wistful, yearning in her voice.

"Maria was the one who introduced Ethan and me to you at her party when you were both started nursing school."

She nods. "I remember."

"What ever happened to her?"

"Got married, and moved to Colorado. We're Facebook friends, and she came back for the funeral. But with busy lives, we don't get to spend too much time together."

I go quiet for a long time as she flips the pages, and looks over the photos. Finally, I break the silence. "Did you go through Ethan's stuff?"

"Yeah," she gestures toward the tote. "I'm keeping those things. Some keepsakes for Chase." I take a look around the room, assess how many trips I'll have to take to Goodwill. Fallon closes the book, and her eyes go wide as she looks at me. "Tell me you are not humming the alligator song?" she says.

"Mother fucker, I am," I say, and she bursts out laughing. "It's the worst."

"The worst," she agrees. "We listened to it on repeat from Spokane to Seattle the other day."

"And you're still sane?" I ask, warmth pushing back the sadness as her laughter curls around me.

"I'm not sure if I ever was to begin with," she says and I chuckle with her.

We both go quiet again and I break it with, "Want to get out of here?"

She shakes her head no. "I have to get this place—"

"After we get the place ready. Let's get out of here, and take Chase to the ocean." I shouldn't be pushing for this. I really shouldn't be. My plan was not to get too close again, not to let this family trust in me, when I'm not a guy who can be trusted. Plus being around her is fucking with me, urging me to give in to the things I feel, but I can't. I can't risk my heart. Not anymore. "You don't want to be here when John starts showing the place," I say forcing the issue. "Katee and Luke will be there. So will Nina and Cole with their son Brandon. You remember them, don't you?"

What are you doing, dude?

She nods. "I remember them from the barbecue you threw a while back."

"Zander's wife Sam, and Jonah's wife Quinn are flying in with the guys. They both have kids and I'm sure they'd love to meet you and Chase."

"Okay." She lets out a breath. "Yeah, let's do it. I can look for a day care when we get back. Chase has been through a lot and I think it will be good for him."

"Okay, good," I say. "I'll let Cole know." I glance around the room, note the cell phone in a plastic bag inside the tote with her keepsakes. I swallow hard when I recognize it as Ethan's phone, still in the hospital bag with his watch, ring and a few other belongings that were on his person when he died. "We can still find a daycare. We can spend the next week getting the house ready, and I know Mom would be happy to garden, and we can check out daycares before we go."

What is with all the 'we'?

"I guess that's a good idea."

She gives me a smile that might just hold a measure of hope for a better future and I give her a squeeze and say, "Why don't you take your drink and go downstairs? I'm going to get to work here."

"Okay, thanks, Jamie."

"Fallon—"

She plants on hand on her hip. "Why don't you like me saying that?"

I give an exaggerated exhale. "If you want to know the truth, it makes me want to fuck you," I say bluntly.

Her eyes go wide and her beautiful breasts bounce and pull my attention when her chest heaves. "Oh. I thought we weren't doing that anymore."

"We're not," I say, but when she wets her lips, my cock twitches in heated anticipation. "You should go, drink your latte, otherwise..."

She hesitates for a moment, turns her back to me and as she walks out the door, I hear her whisper, "Thanks, Jamie."

Motherfucker.

FALLON

Fallon

"I'm going swimming. I'm going swimming. I'm going swimming," Chase says on repeat as Jamie drives my SUV to the cottage on the shore.

He takes a sip of his coffee and sets it back in the console. "I don't know what's worse. His chanting or the damn alligator song."

He casts me a quick glance and when I smile, we both say, "Alligator song." Laughing together, his hand slides across the seat and captures mine. I absorb his warmth, take comfort in his touch. It's been a long time since I've been able to laugh, and after getting the house and gardens ready, the pool cleaned and alarm system installed, not to mention finding Chase an excellent daycare, I can't help but feel a new lightness inside me.

I still have a few weeks off before I go back to work, and my realtor is lining up smaller homes for me to view when I get back from this much needed vacation. Now for the next week, I can just sit back, relax and enjoy the ocean with my son, and my rock-solid best friend. A guy who I have not been to bed with again, and I must say, it's not because I don't want to sleep with him. There's no denying I want his touch again, want to feel him inside my body, and I'm pretty sure his father picked up on the tension between us while he was helping us get the house ready for sale. I can't imagine he'd be too happy with either one of us. But what he doesn't understand is that things weren't good between Ethan and me, and Ethan was most likely hiding things—big things. I'm not sure what I would have done or said if Barry had come right out and asked if there was something going on between Jamie and me.

Will his friends pick up on the tension too?

Heck, maybe we should sleep together again, just to clear the air, and tamp down this insane sexual tension before I burst into a million tiny pieces.

"Something on your mind?" he asks.

I give him a coy grin. "Maybe."

He arches his brow and eyes me. "And you're not telling me why?"

"Maybe I'll tell you later." I gesture with a nod over my shoulder. "When little ears aren't listening."

He casts me a sidelong glance, his eyes narrowing. "Am I going to like it?"

"I think so," I say. Yes, okay we agreed not to sleep together again. We don't want to ruin our friendship and he is my brother-in-law, but maybe while we're on vacation for this next week, we can take a vacation from real life too. Things can go back to normal when we get home and as soon as hockey season starts again, I'm sure he'll be back in bed with all his bunnies. Until then, however...

"I don't like that grin, Fallon. You're up to something," he says, and I reach for my latte and take a sip.

"When did you get so paranoid?" I ask as I lick the foam from my lips and note the way Jamie is watching.

"When did you get so secretive?"

"When did you start answering questions with questions?" I laugh and whack him. He captures my hand, and feigns hurt as he holds it against his hard stomach.

He gestures with his chin, and I glance out the window. "We're here."

As I sit up a little straighter, Chase screams, "We're here, we're here. Mommy, we're here."

I laugh and shake my head. "I think someone is happy to be here."

"Are you?" he asks, his voice holding a measure of seriousness.

"I am," I say. "Thanks Jamie." I bit my lip to stop myself from grinning when he clenches his jaw, the muscles rippling as he growls.

Hmm, maybe I won't have a talk with him. Maybe I'll have a little fun with him, tease him until he's ready to break from frustration. With that delicious thought in mind, I glance around, taking in the rows of amazing homes, the kids, families, and dogs playing on the sand, or in the water, as the midday sun beats down on them.

"This is amazing," I whisper, incredulous. "Wait, did you ever buy a place here, I remember..."

"No, it never happened, but Rider is in Belize with his latest. This is his place, and now ours for the week," he says, parking in front of a beachside mansion.

"This is a cottage?"

Jamie laughs. "I know, right? Pretty nice. Come on, let's get settled and I'll introduce you to everyone."

I know most of the guys from watching the team, met many of them in person at Jamie's place, but I've not yet met Samantha, or Quinn, or any of their children. Daisy is a little older than Chase, Brandon and Scotty a bit young, but I'm sure they're going to get along great.

"Mommy, Mommy, let me out," Chase says, kicking the back of my seat as I open my door and climb out. A warm briny breeze washes over me, and the last of the tension drains from my body as laughter curls around me. I help Chase from his seat, and drop to my knees to have a talk to him.

"Now remember what I said, Chase. You can't run off alone. This is a big place, and the ocean is dangerous. You have to have an adult with you at all times, okay?"

Nodding, he shades the sun from his eyes, and glances out over the water. "Mommy, look," he yells as a huge black dog comes running toward us. I shriek and shove Chase behind me, but Jamie comes up to us and drops to his knees to intervene.

"He's friendly," he says as the dog leaps into his arms, knocking him backward. Chase laughs, and Jamie rubs the dog's ears. "Huxley, what kind of greeting is that?" he asks the excited dog, who is wiggling and wagging his tail so hard he's practically spinning in a circle.

"I want to pet Huxley," Chase yells. "Mommy, I want a dog."

"Come here, bud," Jamie says and holds the dog still so Chase can pet him. My heart stalls as I watch the two, and even though Jamie has no idea, he's been such a positive role model for Chase. Before we even came to the beach, he purchased fishing supplies, floaty toys, and buckets and shovels. He would have been such a great dad.

My heart squeezes at that thought, and my throat tightens. There are things I know—suspect—but I could never, ever in a million years tell Jamie. He's been hurt enough, and my suspicions would destroy him.

"About time you got here." I glance up to see Cole Cannon—The Playmaker—and he's grinning as he wrestles Huxley off Jamie. "Go play, boy," he says, and the dog runs off to the sun-washed beach to play as Cole holds his hand out to me.

"Fallon, I'm so glad you decided to come." He pulls me to my feet and I brush sand from my backside. "The girls can't wait to say hello, and I know the kids have been waiting to play with Chase."

"I'm looking forward to catching up with everyone," I say.

"Barbecue and bonfire tonight, outside my place. Potluck. Hope you guys can make it," Cole says.

"That sounds like a lot of fun," I say. "Jamie bought a ton of food, so I'll make some salads."

"I want pancakes." I glance at Chase as he crinkles his nose at my salad suggestion.

"A man after my own heart," Cole says as he ruffles Chase's too-long hair. "Jesus, he looks like you, Jamie," he says.

"Poor kid," a male voice says, coming up behind Cole.

Cole turns and shoves Luke—the hockey player known as the Stick Handler—and they get into a wrestling match right in the sandy driveway. I roll my eyes at their antics, but I secretly love the comradery between all these hockey players. They're all good guys, with hearts of gold.

"Are you two at it again?" Zander, the player known as the Hard Hitter asks, and peels them off each other. "Fallon, it's nice to see you again. Don't mind these two. They've been off the ice too long and have a lot of pent up aggression."

I totally understand the pent-up thing, but mine isn't aggression. It's passion. Though I think it's best to keep that to myself.

The guys continue to shove one another as another player joins us. I recognize him as the Body Checker. "Nice to see you, Fallon," he says.

I nod, vaguely remember meeting Jonah and a few of the other players at the funeral. All the guys came, but at the time, I'd been walking around in a daze, that whole month is nothing but a blur to me.

"It's nice to see you again too, Jonah." I glance down. "Do you guys all remember, Chase?"

"Oh, yeah," Jonah says. "He's getting big."

Cole drops to one knee, meeting Chase on eye level. "I hear you like to go swimming."

Chase jumps up and down. "I do. I do. I do. Mommy, I want to go swimming."

"Well if it's okay with your mom, while she's getting unpacked, maybe I can take you down to the water. Brandon, Daisy, and Scotty are all playing and swimming."

"Mommy, can I? Can I?" Chase asks.

I feel a measure of unease. Cole is a good father and good man, but Chase doesn't know him and since he lost his dad, I've been a little overprotective.

Jamie casts me a quick glance. He angles his head, assesses me, and says, "I know I could use a swim."

I smile at him. "Thanks Jamie," I say on purpose, and every muscle in his body stiffens. I nibble my bottom lip and he goes perfectly still for a moment, and I get the sense he's figured out that I'm messing with him.

"Yeah, okay," he says through gritted teeth and scrubs his face. "Where are the water wings?"

"I'll get them." I open the back of the SUV and hand over sunscreen and water wings.

"Thanks, Fallon," he says, his eyes latched on my mouth as I lick my parched lips.

"Swim. Swim. Swim," Chase screams, and Jamie scoops him up.

"The door is open. Just head on in," Cole says.

"I will," I say and pull my phone from my back pocket. I take a picture of the ocean, and post it on Instagram. I haven't used my account in a long time, but being here has inspired me to get back amongst the living.

The guys turn to go, and I nearly burst out laughing when I hear Jamie ask, "Have you guys ever heard of the alligator song?"

Moans and groans from the guys reach my ears and I laugh some more as I pull groceries, suitcases and beach bags from the SUV and start carrying them into the house. Laughter from the kids playing follows me and fills me with joy. For a while there I never thought I'd laugh again, and I must say, I think this trip is just what Chase needs.

I walk through the place, take in the beach decor, furnishings and enjoy the warm breeze blowing in through the open windows. I go upstairs and check out the bedrooms and bathrooms—yes there are more than one bathroom in this beachside cottage, aka mansion—and walk into the master suite which looks out over the water. I pull the curtain back and smile when I see Jamie and Chase in the distance. Chase is jumping up and down, having a hard time getting into the water. It's not pool temperature like he's used to.

"Hello," someone calls out from downstairs.

"I'm up here," I say. "Be right down."

I make my way back downstairs to find Katee and Nina, along with two other women I've never met. Dressed in a bathing suit with a knitted cover up thrown over it, Katee pulls me in for a hug. Then Nina, who is also dressed in her suit, takes a turn.

"This is Sam, Zander's wife," Katee says, introducing me to the other women. "And this is Quinn. Zander's sister and Jonah's wife."

Quinn holds up a bottle of wine. "And this is Pinot Noir," she says, and we all laugh.

"Let's go find some glasses," I say and lead them into the kitchen.

"I know where they are." Nina opens the cupboard to pull out the stemware, as Katee pulls a cork screw from the drawer.

"You guys know your way around this place," I say.

"We should. We decorated it for Rider," Katee says.

Nina grins. "That's right. If it wasn't for us, you'd be sitting on a lawn chair."

"I did note the place has a woman's soft touch. It was so nice of Rider to lend it to us."

"He's off with his latest, on vacation in Belize," Nina says and rolls her eyes.

"You don't like her?" I ask, confused.

"We don't know her," Nina explains. "He doesn't keep a woman around long enough."

"We need to get the Wing Man married," Katee says with a sad shake of her head.

"I always liked him," I say.

Katee smiles at me. "So, you and Jamie," she says, almost like we're an item. I'm about to correct her but she adds, "I'm so glad you could make it. We haven't been able to get Jamie out here." In a softer voice she says, "The guys worry about him. We do too."

I give her a warm smile. I love how they all take care of each other, and this last year, Jamie really needed his friends. "Coming here was actually his idea," I say and accept the glass of wine from Quinn. As I look at her I can see the resemblance to her brother Zander. "I wasn't sure I could make it at first. We had a lot to do to get my place on the market."

"Jamie's been helping with things?" Katee asks, and toys with her wine cup.

"I'd be lost without him," I say, and Nina gives me a smile. "And he's a good role model for Chase."

"I haven't seen him this happy in a long time," Nina says.

"You're clearly good for him." Her gaze skims over me and she nods. "You look good, too, Fallon."

"Thanks," I say, trying not to think about the way Jamie worshipped my body, gave me back a measure of my confidence.

"I'd say Jamie's been good for you too," Katee says and for some unknown reason my cheeks heat. Okay, well, maybe the reason really isn't that unknown. Maybe it's because I can't stop thinking about our beautiful night together, and how much I want it to happen again. The truth is, we're both single consenting adults and if we want to take pleasure in each other's bodies, and keep our emotions out of it, why not?

"Oh, it's like that is it?" Katee says laughing. "Well done, Fallon. Jamie is quite the catch, and you two look good together. You always were close."

"No, no, no," I say and take a drink of wine to cover my embarrassment. "We're just…" What am I supposed to say, oh we've only had sex once but I plan on changing that tonight?

"Girlfriend, your secret is in the vault," Nina says and lifts her glass in salute and everyone takes a drink, everyone except Katee. "Unless you want to give me fodder for my next hot hockey romance novel."

"Hell no," I say quickly, and everyone laughs.

"It was worth a shot," she says with a shrug. "Okay, let's all go join the guys for a swim."

I set my glass down, loving how accepting these women are, and how they're not jumping to judge me for sleeping with Jamie. "I need to get changed."

"We'll wait," Quinn says.

I hurry upstairs, dig into my bag for my suit and tug it on. I glance at my curves in the mirror and remember how much Jamie loved seeing me in this suit. I grab a towel, but before I head back downstairs, my cell phone rings.

I grab it and check the caller ID, but it says private number and it takes me back to the day I got the call in my kitchen, when no one was on the other end. I slide my finger across the screen.

"Hello."

A long pause and then, "Fallon?"

My heart jumps into my throat. "Sara. Ohmigod is that you?" I ask and sink down onto the soft mattress.

"I...uh, heard you were back in Seattle," she says, sounding a bit breathless.

"I am. Where are you?" I ask.

"How is Jamie?" she asks instead of answering me.

"He's...about as good as can be expected," I say. Truthfully, he's doing a lot better than the first night I came home. As my mind reels, everything inside me urges me to ask her about her relationship with Ethan, but I can't formulate the words as my heart crashes against my too tight chest.

"Are you with him?" she asks.

Had she seen my Instagram post?

"I...well, we're at Rider's cottage on the ocean."

A long pause and then, "I loved him, you know." I'm about to ask who she loved, Ethan or Jamie, when a crash comes from downstairs. I jump from the bed, phone still in hand. But the line is now dead.

"Sara?" I stare at the phone as laughter reaches my ears. I take a couple deep breaths and drop my phone onto the bedding, my heart and mind still racing. Why would Sara reach out to me now? Is she upset that I'm here with Jamie? I mean, she's the one who left him, and who exactly did she mean when she said she loved him? With those thoughts bouncing around inside my rattled brain, I head back downstairs and find Katee cleaning up a broken wine glass.

"Nina's a lightweight," she says. "She's cut off."

Nina shakes her head. "It was an accident." But then her

eyes narrow. "Are you okay? You look like you've seen a ghost."

"Oh, I'm fine," I say quickly. "I just didn't know what happened."

That explanation seems to satisfy her as she hands Katee the dustpan. Once the mess is cleaned up, we all go outside and make our way down the beach. As I walk toward Jamie, his gaze falls over me, taking me in from the top of my head to the bottom of my toes. The women I'm with are slim and beautiful, and I can't help but feel a little thrill when Jamie only seems to have his eyes on me. My heart does a little flip and I quickly remind myself to keep this about sex. I walk up to him, and his gaze narrows as it moves over my face.

"You okay?" he asks, and I stare at him for a second. I have no idea whether to tell him Sara called or not. Will he be happy that I heard from her, or will it bring back too many memories and ruin this vacation for him. "Fallon?"

"Fine," I say. "I just had a glass of wine with the girls and with this heat, I think it went to my head."

"This will sober you up," he says and picks me up. "And cool you down."

"Put me down," I yell, and Chase and the kids start laughing.

"Nope."

I pound on his chest, but can't seem to stop laughing. "Jamie, I mean it."

Cole grabs Nina and she starts yelping. "Don't even think about it, Cole," Nina yells, but she's laughing too. Soon enough all the guys have their wives in their arms and the kids are jumping up and down and yelling and laughing. It warms my soul, and for the first time in a long time, has me believing I can once again find my normal.

I just want it with Jamie.

Oh boy!

Jamie carries me out into the cold water. When the waves reach his stomach, he goes to his knees, taking me down with him. "It's freezing," I scream and try to climb onto his shoulders. "You're going to pay for this."

"You looked like you needed to cool off." His grin is playful. "You should be *thanking* me, don't you think," he says, with an arch of his brow. Oh yeah, he's totally on to me, and from the look on his face, I'm guessing he isn't opposed to the idea of sleeping together again. I'm not sure what changed his mind—maybe it was the incredible tension between us this last week—I only know I'm glad he's on board. "Do you have any idea what you're doing to me right now?" he grumbles low into my ear.

"Meaning?"

"This bathing suit. Fuck, Fallon. I needed to get in the water to cover my hard-on before everyone sees it."

"So that's what this was all about?" I say and slide my hand down, beneath the water where no one can see, to cup his erection.

"Mommy," Chase says, and I push off Jamie. He ducks under and swims out as I wade back in and plunk myself down on the sand next to my son. The women all swim back in as the guys follow Jamie out.

Breathing hard, Nina drops down next to me and her son Brandon runs circles around us. She gives me a nudge with her shoulder. "So, you and Jamie," she says with a huge smile.

"We're just friends," I inform her.

"Friends with benefits." She winks at me. "Like Katee and Luke were, and look how that turned out."

"Wait, what?"

JAMIE

I've been walking around with the worst fucking hard-on since seeing Fallon in her bathing suit this afternoon. Okay, maybe that's not entirely true. The boner started when we were in the car and she *thanked* me. At first I thought she was just being her sincere self, but when I caught her nibbling on her bottom lip, it occurred to me that she was fucking with me. Oh, yeah, she knows what those two words do to me, and she said them on purpose.

Motherfucker.

I should stay away tonight. I should get back in the SUV and drive straight to my place, lock the door and never come out again. But am I going to do that? Fuck no. Seeing the smile on Fallon's face, watching her come alive again, especially under my touch last week, is not something I can bring myself to run from, even though it's exactly what I should be doing. But I want her happy, and if having sex again with me makes her happy, then who am I to deny her? Just as long as we're both clear it's just sex, and can never be anything more.

As we sit around the bonfire, day bleeding into night, Fallon sips wine and chats with the women as they all help the kids roast marshmallows. I take a sip of beer from my bottle and let it dangle from my fingers. Beside me, Cole gives me a nudge.

"Fallon fits right in," he says.

"Yeah," I mumble, unable to take my eyes off the way her shirt clings to her breasts and her frayed shorts show off her beautiful legs, legs I plan to have wrapped around my head tonight.

"How long have you been sleeping with her?"

My gaze jerks to Cole so fast my neck nearly snaps. I catch the smirk playing on his face and shake my head. "Fuck man, are you looking to be laid out with another concussion?"

Cole laughs. "Come on, Jamie. The tension between you two is explosive. Did you think we weren't going to notice?"

"I was hoping." I swing my bottle in my fingers before I take another sip. "She's my sister-in-law," I say.

"What's that got to do with anything?"

"She was my brother's wife," I say.

"Only because he claimed her first."

"What the fuck, man?" Jesus, am I that transparent to Cole, to the others...to my parents? Does everyone know that I've always wanted Fallon as more than a friend? But now, after the accident, even though we're both single, there can't be more between us. I don't want to let her down, hurt her more than she's been hurt.

Cole relaxes in his lawn chair, kicks his legs out and crosses his feet at the ankles. Once he's comfortable, he says, "Just calling it as I see it."

"I was engaged to another woman, remember?"

"And now you're not."

"No, I'm not." I wanted to do right by Sara when she got pregnant, and I liked her a lot. But did I love her? Would I ever be able to love a woman the way I love Fallon?

Fuck me.

Chase shrieks when his marshmallow catches on fire, and I can't take my eyes from Fallon's mouth when she blows it out. I shift, uncomfortable in my shorts and Cole, bastard that he is, chuckles beside me.

"You two are good together," he says.

"We're not having this conversation." I finish the beer and reach into the cooler and grab two more. I twist the caps off and hand one to Cole.

"I'm just saying. She can't keep her eyes off you. You can't keep your eyes off her. You guys have been pretty good friends over the years."

"That's all we are, Cole. Friends. We can't be anything more than that. I'm not the guy for her."

"Okay, then. Maybe I'll give Kane a call. She's definitely his type."

Once again, my head snaps around and I glare at Cole. He laughs and shakes his head. "Yeah, that's what I thought."

"Kane's not the guy for her. Besides she's not ready for more. She made that perfectly clear."

"Maybe not." He goes quiet and I think he's going to let the subject drop until he leans into me again and say, "Remember the playoffs, our seventh game with Detroit?"

"How could I forget? We won the cup that night."

He nods and smile. "Yeah we did, thanks to you."

"Team effort," I say.

"It was your goal in overtime that sealed the deal."

I shrug.

"Jesus, that was a risky move you took that night, could have gone bad but in the end, it paid off."

"I know what you're doing, Cole," I say and take a long pull from the bottle. "But my risk-taking days are behind me."

"Too bad, because Fallon is an amazing woman. I know you think so too. You talked about her enough over the years." His gaze narrows in on me. "And I wouldn't want you to miss your shot with her because you blame yourself for what happened. It wasn't your fault, Jamie."

My grip on my bottle tightens. "There are things you don't know."

"Maybe there are things you don't know too," he says and as I glare at him, my stomach squeezing.

"What are you talking about?" I ask my mind going back to a conversation I had with Fallon, and how I thought she was keeping things from me.

"I'm not saying anything." He takes a big drink. "Too much beer," he says, but I'm not so sure I believe him. "All I know is sometimes we need to take risks, and you deserve happiness."

As I stare at him I can't help but wonder if he knows something I don't? If he does, why would he keep secrets from me? We're buddies, teammates. Ending the conversation, Cole stands and goes and sits by Nina.

"Daddy, Daddy," Brandon says, as he shoves another marshmallow onto the stick.

Daisy runs up to Zander. "Daddy, do you want one?"

"You bet," Zander says as Scotty starts running in circles from the sugar high.

"Come here, kiddo," Jonah says. "No more sugar for you."

"More, Daddy more," he says and that's when I note the way Chase is looking around, his tired eyes wide as he watches the men interact with their children. My heart squeezes, and while I'm not his father, not about to even pretend I am—I'm the fucking reason he doesn't have one—I climb from my seat and sit in front of the fire with him. I cross my legs, and get comfortable on the ground.

"How about roasting one for me?" I say to him and the smile that comes over his face is like a fist to the gut. As Chase sticks the marshmallow into the flames, Luke stands up.

"Okay, I have something to say," he announces. Katee grins at him, and he pulls her to her feet. She wraps her arms around him, and he holds her close.

All eyes turn to them, as they stand there grinning. "I'd just like to point out that soon enough, we're going to have enough kids to form our own hockey team," Luke says, and puts his hand on his wife's stomach.

"No way," Nina says and jumps up. "You're pregnant Katee?"

Katee puts her hand on her stomach, over Luke's, and Fallon turns to look at me. Her eyes are soft, sincere as her gaze moves over my face. No doubt she's wondering if Katee's announcement has taken me back, reminding me of the baby I lost? Fallon knows me well enough to understand it's a wound that won't heal. I just hope Sara has moved on, found someone better than me.

But in this moment, I'm happy for my friends, thrilled. In confidence, Luke told me ages ago they'd been trying to get pregnant, and I don't want to bring the mood down, so I give her a smile to let her know I'm okay. The truth is, being with Fallon, seeing her smile again, is somehow helping me become whole again. But I don't deserve that. I don't deserve her.

"That's right," Katee says, and I focus my attention back on her. "We're having a baby. I'm three months along. We were waiting for everyone to be together to tell you."

The girls squeal loudly and all jump up to hug her, while the guys pat Luke on the back. Luke pulls a bottle of champagne from his cooler and cracks the lid. Katee hands out small plastic glasses and Luke fills them. We all salute them and swallow the champagne like it's a shot.

"That's why you weren't drinking this afternoon," Sam says, shaking her head. "Or now."

Katee holds up her can of soda. "That's right."

"How do you get a baby?" Daisy asks her mom Sam, and we all go silent, save for Cole chuckling beside me. "Can we get a baby?"

"Oh boy. Thanks a lot, Katee," Sam says and we all laugh when she rolls her eyes. She turns to Daisy. "We'll talk about that later okay. Right now, I think it's time for bed."

"I don't want to go to bed," Daisy says.

"Your bedtime too, Chase," Fallon says. The women gather up their tired, and grumbling kids. I take Chase's stick and set it beside the fire pit, and climb to my feet.

"I think I'll call it a night too," I say, and avoid eye contact with Cole as he snorts.

As the group parts, off to tuck their kids in for the night, I step up to Fallon, and walk her and Chase back to the house. Our knuckles brush, and a bolt of lust zaps my balls. Dammit, I abused my cock more times in the last week than I have in my entire life. It's a wonder I can fucking walk straight. Everything in me knows it's wrong to take comfort from Fallon when I don't deserve it, but she does. She deserves the world, so I'll keep my shit together and give her everything she needs this week.

Chase drags his feet, and Fallon picks him up. "He's beat."

"Here let me." I take Chase from her and he sets his chin on my shoulder. She opens her mouth, and I know exactly what she's going to say, so I cut her off. "Before you say anything, you're welcome," I say, and she laughs quietly.

"I'm really glad we came here." She exhales with a happy sigh. "It's good for Chase."

"And you, Fallon? Is it good for you too?" Her shoulders have relaxed. They're no longer touching her ears, but I just want to hear it from her.

Her hands slides around my back, and the warmth of her touch goes right through me. "I think it's going to be *great* for me," she says, and I get that we're talking about something else entirely now, something that involves the two of us naked, and a warm bed.

With that last thought in mind, I hurry my steps and when we reach the house, she opens the door and I take Chase upstairs. He stirs in my arms and rubs his tired eyes.

"Can you set him on the bathroom sink," Fallon says quietly. "He needs to wash up and brush his teeth."

I carry him into the bathroom, and Fallon reaches for his toothbrush and toothpaste as I set him onto the counter.

"I'm going to jump in the shower," I say, needing to rinse the salty ocean from my skin. She nods, a small smile playing on her mouth like she's up to no good—damned if I don't like that. I strip off as I make my way to the master suite bathroom. I turn on the water, adjust the temperature and climb in. I moan as the needle-like spray falls from the rain shower. I stand under it for a long time, and my cock grows thicker as I think about having Fallon in my arms again, putting my mouth all over her lush body. Eyes pinched tight, I reach for my cock, give it a couple tugs, and a low moan catches in my throat.

"Need a hand?"

My lids flutter open, and my cock grows impossibly thicker when a naked Fallon steps into the shower with me.

"Fuck yeah," I say. I reach for her, and none too gently pull her against me. Then another thought hits. "Wait, what about—"

"He's fast asleep, which means it's our playtime now." She runs her finger over my chest and circles my nipple.

"You want to play with me, Fallon?"

She grins, and takes my cock into her hands. I breathe in the enticing, heady scent of her arousal as she rubs the long length of me as she says, "I've been wanting to do this all week."

"Me too," I growl and push her wet hair from her shoulders. I touch her chin, lift it until we're eye to eye. "I want to keep fucking you, Fallon, but you need to know——"

"I know," she says. "This is just sex."

With that, she drops to her knees and takes my cock into her mouth. I lean forward to keep the spray off her as she works me to the back of her throat, taking me deeper than she did last time. I grab a fistful of her hair, and pull it to the side so I can watch her take me in.

"You are so beautiful," I say, and she cups my balls, gives them a soft massage. Need and lust fry my last working brain cell, and her soft moans of delight as she cherishes my cock prompt me into action. I pull her off me, and she slides up my body as I put my hand between her legs to find her warm and wet for me.

"I don't know how I made it through the week," I say, my breathing coming a bit faster. "All I could think about was getting my mouth on you again."

"The girls know about us," she says as I insert a finger. "They don't seem to have a problem with us being together. They were actually happy about it."

"Yeah, the guys know too. I couldn't stop staring at you tonight, and fucking Cole called me out on it." She chuckles, but it turns into a moan as I slide my finger in and out of her and fuck her slowly. "He talked about setting you up with Kane."

"Really, that's odd."

"Yeah, well, don't worry, I told him you weren't interested. You're not, are you?" I ask, not sure if I want to hear the answer. "I mean, Kane's a good guy but——"

"No. I don't want to date anyone, Jamie."

I ignore the relief racing through me. She can be with Kane if she wants. Hell, she can be with any guy, but dammit, the thoughts of another man's hands on her body doesn't sit right with me.

"I told him you weren't ready for more," I say, and press my mouth to the hollow of her throat. I breathe in her warm scent. "You're not, right?"

What the... Why am I asking her that?

Oh, maybe because you're checking to see if she changed her mind.

But goddammit, I can't be the guy for her. Even though I know that, I suddenly can't stop thinking about it.

Fucking Cole!

"No, I'm not," she murmurs, and I slide another finger inside her for a snug fit. She's so responsive and warm and wet I can barely think straight. Her nails score my skin. "That is so good." I pull my fingers out, grip her shoulders and turn her.

"Okay, enough talking. It's time to fuck," I say, my cock harder than it's ever been before. "Put your hands here." I press her palms to the tiled wall, and I stand back to look at her perfect body. I'm not sure I've ever wanted a woman more.

"Jamie, please," she murmurs and wiggles her ass at me. I put my foot between her legs and widen them and her sweet plump curves jut out even more. I take a palm full of her lush ass and squeeze.

"My cock is so hard," I say and take it in my hand. I run it along her crevice and she wiggles some more. "I nearly came in your mouth a minute ago."

"Maybe I would have liked that," she says, and I growl. I love how free and open she is with me. It reminds me of old times when we used to hang out, say anything we wanted. Although that's not entirely true. There were secrets I kept. Things I'd never say to my brother's girl.

"You know, I never knew you were such a fucking tease."

"Well, I did tell you I'd get payback for dunking me this afternoon."

"And payback is telling me you want my cum in your mouth."

"No, that was true. Payback comes later, when I widen my legs on the bed, and put my fingers into my hot, wet pussy, and torture you by making you watch without touching."

I exhale harshly. "Fuck Fallon."

"Yes, fuck me, Jamie. I want your cock inside me."

She pushes her ass against my cock and I reach around her, brush my thumb over her clit, visualizing her on the bed, playing with herself. "Promise me you'll do that later?"

"Yeah, Jamie. I'll do that for you."

I let out a breath I didn't even realize I was holding as she bucks against my hand. "Fuck," I murmur. Her responsiveness, and neediness fuck me over big time. I love the way she wants me. Her body grows hotter as I hold her curvy hips, position my cock at her entrance and say, "I want you so fucking much, this is going to be fast and hard."

"Yes," she cries out.

"Next time. Next time, I'll go slower, but this last week had been torturous, and right now I need to fuck hard and fill you with my cum."

Her breathing grows choppy, and I hold her hips for leverage and I piston forward, and bury myself high inside her. Steam fills the room, making it harder and harder to get air. Then again, maybe my lack of breath has less to do with the steam and more to do with Fallon and being inside her like this. Her muscles clench around me, and I can't believe how close she already is. Then again, so am I.

"You needed my cock, baby, didn't you?"

"Yes." Her sharp, needy cries of pleasure wrap around my cock, and pull me under until I'm drowning in sensation.

"I shouldn't have denied you," I say. "I should have been fucking you all week. Making you scream my name, and giving you orgasm after orgasm." My cock swells and she feels so damn good I can barely focus. Christ I've wanted this for so long. Wanted her. But Ethan moved in on her while I was away. Did he know? Did he know what she meant to me?

"It should have been me," I say without thinking, my voice a deep husky breath. I pound into her hard, fast, blunt, like a man on a mission, a man determined to stake his claim, but I can't get deep enough, can't get enough of her. Her cries of ecstasy curl around me, and her fingers scratch against the wall.

"Jamie," she cries out and I lean over her, dig my fingers into her hips hard enough to bruise her. But I can't seem to help myself, can't seem to get high enough, even though I'm balls fucking deep. "Yes," she cries out. "Hard, just like that."

I pound into her, deep strokes that nearly slam her against the wall. Her cries of pleasure curl around me, a telltale sign she likes my frenzied fucking, and it's a good thing, because I'd never want to do anything to hurt her, yet I can't seem to get myself under control. I'm seriously losing my shit big time, and if I'm not careful, I might drown with everything I feel for this incredible woman, but have been tamping down since the day I met her.

"You like this, Fallon. You like me fucking you like this?" I ask, wanting to hear her say it.

"Yes," she huffs out, her body quivering in my hands, around my cock as I fill her. "I want all your cum in me." Her fingers curl. "Oh, Jamie. I'm coming. It's so good." Her hot juice coats my dick and drips over my balls, and my cock throbs with the need for release, but I don't want to come just yet, I want to stay buried inside of her like this for the rest of the night.

Forever.

"That is so fucking good," I say as her muscles squeeze and massage my dick. "Ride my cock. Use it, Fallon. Fill that sweet pussy and take what you need." I pull out, slam back in again, and before I know it, she's coming again. My chest puffs up, proud that I can wring two orgasms out of her sweet body. Later, I plan to go for a third.

But I can't think about that anymore. No, right now all I can do is think about the pleasure centered between my legs and how I'm going to blow before I want to. "I'm there, baby. I'm right there."

"Fill me, Jamie. Fill me with your cum," she cries out and I fall over her, slide my hands around her ribcage and cup her breasts as I let go on a deep, gasping breath. Her muscles continue to wreck my cock as I spurt my seed high inside her. I go deeper, not wanting any to drip out, and loving the idea of her feeling it dribble out of her tight pussy later. I completely deplete myself, and breathe hard against her back as I work to regain focus.

When my world rights itself, I pull out of her, and walk backwards with her until her limp body is under the hot spray. With her back to my chest, she lets her head fall to my shoulder, and as I catch her contented smile, I grab the soap and later her sated body.

"That...that was incredible," she says, her voice a breathless whisper.

"No, babe," I say, and she stiffens. "That wasn't just incredible, that was just the start of the night. Now what was it you said about payback?"

FALLON

I wake to the sound of children playing on the beach and roll over to find the other side of the bed empty. I slide my hand across and touch the cool mattress. A quick glance at the clock lets me know it's still early. Jamie must have snuck out ages ago, and while I miss his heat and comfort, it's for the best. I don't want to give Chase the wrong idea. Or the right idea.

Oh, God.

Last night with Jamie was amazing, of that I have no doubt. The way he touched me, kissed me, it was just so damn hard to remember this is a temporary thing, and that we're just enjoying each other's bodies for the rest of the week. I swallow against the storm of emotions tossing wildly in my stomach.

"It should have been me."

I sit up in the bed, trying to wrap my brain around those words spoken in the heat of passion. Truthfully, I'd been so lost in him I'm still not sure I heard him right. I slide out from beneath the sheets, tug on my frayed shorts and a T-shirt, and walk to the window. A smile touches my mouth when I spot the guys on the beach with their kids. My heart pinches, knowing Chase is the only one without a father, but I can't go down that road again. I won't.

Unless it was with Jamie.

Oh boy, I really am in trouble here. I told him last night I wasn't interested in more, but it was a bold-faced lie. I can't come out and tell him what I feel. He made it clear twice now that this is just about sex and I don't want to ruin our friendship. Chase needs him in his life as much as I do, and I can't risk losing him.

As I take in the scene on the beach, I can only assume Jamie snuck into another bedroom and Chase is still asleep at this early hour, but when I scan the beach, I find them both jogging, Jamie's pace slow so Chase can keep up. My heart jumps into my throat. Yeah, telling Jamie how I feel, and risk losing him, is a chance I can't take. Chase has had enough loss, and he's growing closer and closer to Jamie by the day.

As if he feels my eyes on him, Jamie glances up into the bedroom. He drops to his knees and points upward. Chase follows the movement, and they both wave emphatically. The room closes in on me as I wave back. Jamie stands and rubs his stomach and I laugh. The man is always hungry.

I close the curtain and make a trip to the bathroom to freshen up and brush my teeth. Once I'm sort of presentable, I head downstairs to start breakfast. Humming the stupid alligator song, I flick on the TV, put it to a music station and head into the kitchen. I pull some bacon, eggs and fruit from the fridge, and go to make coffee but discover the pot is already full.

"Bless you, Jamie," I say.

"Are you praying for me?"

I jump at the sound of Jamie's voice, and turn to see them coming in through the front door. A warm breeze follows them in and carries the enticing scent of Jamie's skin. A shimmer of warmth goes through me.

"Mommy, I went jogging," Chase says and runs his hand across his forehead, mimicking Jamie. It's adorable. He makes a muscle. "I'm going to be big and strong like Jamie."

I touch his arm. "Wow, you're big and strong now."

He makes a motor sound and runs into the other room. "Did he...see us?"

"No, I went into the spare room before sunrise. I heard him get up, and I needed a run, so he came with me."

"Well, now it's my turn to cook breakfast for you two." Jamie comes close, dressed in nothing but his running shorts, his upper body slick and hard and so fine, all I want to do is go up on my toes and kiss him.

"Did you miss me?" he asks playfully.

"You know I did. Did you miss me?"

"Yeah, and I want to kiss you so fucking bad right now," he says, his breath coming a little faster as his gaze drops to my mouth. I look past his shoulder's, and listen to Chase's footsteps climbing the stairs.

"I won't deny you what you want," I tease, and wet my bottom lip in preparation.

He growls, slides one hand around my waist, and drags me to him. His mouth captures mine, and the kiss is slow and soft at first, an easy exploration. But when I sag against him, put my hands on his chest and scratch slightly, it brings out the beast in him. He deepens the kiss, his tongue sliding in to play with mine as he backs me up, presses his hard erection against my body.

After last night, and all the fun we had, it's insane that he's hard again—insane how much I want him again. I guess so many years of pent up passion has turned me into a regular old nymphomaniac. But I don't suspect I'd be this way with anyone but this man.

He angles his head, and claims my mouth with his, stealing the breath from my lungs. Honestly, how can a man who wants only a physical relationship kiss me like that? Like he means it. Like maybe he wants more and doesn't know it.

Okay, Fallon. Cut it out, that's just wishful thinking.

A knock sounds on the door, and we jump apart. I'm breathing hard, my body on fire, my skin flushed, when I ask, "Who could that be?" A sickening knot grips my gut, and for a minute I worry that it's Sara, coming back to patch things up with her man.

Would Jamie want that?

The door flings open and loud chatter reaches my ears as I see the four guys, the four women and the three kids come busting in, carrying delicious smelling casserole dishes and paper bags and juice containers.

"What's going on?" Jamie asks.

"Breakfast," Cole says.

"I was just about to cook," I say, my gaze darting from one person to the other trying to figure out what's going on.

"We have a ton of food here," Katee says, then goes still. "Wait, did Luke forget to tell you that we were all having breakfast here?"

Jamie punches Luke on the arm. "Yeah, he kind of did," Jamie says but he doesn't look like he minds the interruption. I don't either.

"I had other things on my mind, baby," Luke says and pulls her in for a kiss.

"Get a room," Jonah says as pushes passed them. "I'm starving."

"Me, too," Jamie says, and I laugh.

"You're always hungry," I say but when he turns to me, and I catch the promise in his eyes, one that says we'll be finishing what we started here, a fine shiver moves through me.

"I'll go get a shirt on," he says.

"Where's Chase?" Daisy asks, her curls bouncing as she searches the room.

"He's upstairs, come with me and I'll help you find him."

The kids all dash upstairs with Jamie, and Katee sidles up to me. "We weren't catching you at a bad time, were we?"

"No," I say quickly, too quickly, and she laughs.

"You're looking a bit flushed," she says. "If you want us to go, we will and we'll take Chase."

I fan my hand in front of my face, but Katee is no fool. "No. No. It's just hot here at the beach," I explain with a grin, but then my thoughts go back to Sara. Guilt for keeping the phone call from Jamie eats at me. Should I tell him? Heck, Sara was my friend, my confidante. She's the one I'd go to when I was having a dilemma. I can't very well go to her now, and ask what she thinks I should do.

"You might as well put the eggs and bacon away," Quinn says. "The hostess never has to cook and we have enough food here to feed an army."

"Or half the hockey team," Cole says. He reaches in to the cupboard and pulls out a bunch of plates as the women arrange the casserole dishes and remove the covers. "Rider will be pissed that he's missing out."

I reach for the silverware, and Jamie comes back from upstairs and stands next to me. "You okay with all this?"

"Absolutely. It's just been Chase and me for too long. I like your friends, Jamie."

He lightly touches the small of my back. "Okay, good," he says, and I have to say, I like the way he checks in on me.

"I can't say they have good timing, though," I tease with a grin.

"Come on down for breakfast, kids," Luke says, from the bottom of the stairs, and it sounds like a of herd of elephants on the ceiling as the hungry crew come running. We plate food up for the kids and set them up in the living room to watch Paw Patrol while they eat. Once they're settled, we make our plates and sit at the table.

"This all looks amazing," I say and put a dash of salt on my food.

"Tomorrow morning, breakfast at my place," Quinn says and point her thumbs at herself. "I am *not* cooking."

I scoop some scrambled egg onto my fork and slide it into my mouth. "Mmm, delicious," I say and note the way Jamie is watching me eat. There's a hunger in his eyes but it's not for food. A thrill goes through me. Damn, I love the way he stares, the incredible, confident way he makes me feel about myself.

"It's daddy/daughter, daddy/son day," Sam says to me. "That means we're kid-free for the afternoon. We're all going antiquing later. We're hoping you can join us?"

I blink rapidly. "I...I can't. I have Chase. He doesn't have..."

All those around the table go quiet, and Sam's eyes go wide, full of regret. She touches my hand. "I'm sorry. I didn't mean. I was just thinking Jamie..."

Not wanting anyone uncomfortable, I put on a smile and say, "It's okay." I steal a glance at Jamie, who is watching me carefully. My stupid heart beats a little faster as I imagine him stepping into that role. But that's crazy. I only ever wanted him to be a positive role model for Chase. Not a father.

I think...

"I'll take him," Jamie says with a shrug. "I wanted to go fishing this week, so today would be a good day. There's a stocked lake not too far from here. We'll catch dinner for everyone."

"The only thing you'll catch down at the lake is a bunch of fly bites," Luke goads.

Jamie, never one to back down, glares at Luke, his eyes

narrowing in challenge. "Care to put your money where your mouth is?" he shoots back.

"Damn right," Luke says. "Whoever catches the biggest bass wins, and the others cook dinner."

"I think Brandon and I would like to get in on that," Cole says.

"Scotty and I would too," Jonah says.

Zander laughs. "It's not Daisy's thing, but as long as she doesn't have to touch any worms, and I buy her a chocolate ice cream, she'll be happy to come along."

As the conversation turns back to the contest, the men all start telling tales about past fishing experiences. Beneath the table, Jamie's hand lands on my leg, and he gives a squeeze.

My gaze goes to him, and I ask, "You sure you don't mind?"

"Absolutely. Go have fun."

I smile at him and Jonah says, "Get a room."

I shake my head as everyone laughs, and we settle in to finish our meals. The guys start talking hockey, naturally, and I turn to Katee. "Are you looking for baby things today?"

"I am. Although I have to get neutral colors. We're going to wait to find out the baby's sex."

"I did that too," I say and remember back to when Chase was born. Ethan was in the delivery room with me, but Jamie was out in the waiting room, pacing like a crazy man. He was the first to set eyes on his nephew.

"All this talk of pregnancy is making me think," Quinn says and puts her hand over her stomach.

"I know," I say and do the same without even realizing it.

"You thinking of giving Chase a brother or a sister?" Quinn asks me.

"I...no...not really. I'd need a guy for that?" I say jokingly, and from my peripheral vision, catch the way Jamie is looking at me.

I turn the conversation back to Katee and her pregnancy as I finish the food on my plate. Soon enough, our bellies are full, and everyone makes their way home to get ready for the day. I take Chase upstairs to get him washed up and dressed for his first fishing expedition in a stocked lake. I coat him with sunscreen and when Jamie pokes his head into the bathroom, I hold the bottle out to him, "You need this too."

"Yes, Mom," he teases and Chase laughs. I give him a scolding glare as he tugs off his shirt, and my gaze instantly drops to take in his striated muscles, many covered by tattoos. My fingers itch to touch him and I grow warm between the legs as I take my time admiring him. He makes a noise and I lift my eyes, catch his smirk.

Busted.

He coats his hands and rubs the lotion over himself, and I help Chase from the counter. "Go find a ballcap to wear," I say to him. He runs off to his room and Jamie hands me the bottle.

"Would you mind doing my back?"

I squeeze a generous amount on his back and his muscles flex as I rub it in, and cop a feel at the same time. I study his tattoos, and my hands still.

What the hell?

"Jamie..."

"Yeah."

I touch the name on his back, in such small letters that I never caught it before. I trace the letters and he stiffens, like he knows what I'm about to ask. "Why do you have my name on your back?"

His muscles flex, and relax beneath my fingers. "Because I...because you're my friend."

We both go so quiet, I can practically hear my son breathing in the other room. I scan his back, look for Sara's name, but it's nowhere to be found. Shocked, touched, and maybe a little confused, I ask, "When did you get this done?"

"A long time ago," is all he says, and I get the sense he wants to drop the subject.

I go back to rubbing in the lotion and slide my hand down, beneath the band of his shorts to run my palms over his scrumptious ass, and his breathing changes.

"Ah, what are you doing?" he asks.

"Just want to make sure to get all the spots," I say, and take my hand from his shorts when Chase comes running back to us.

"I don't want to touch worms," Chase says and makes a face.

"It's not so bad, bud," Jamie informs him, and my heart nearly bursts with the love I have for these two. "Let's go." Chase darts down the stairs, and Jamie nods to the bottle of lotion in my hand. "Oh, wait, did you need me to rub this on you anywhere?" he teases and leans in for a kiss. It's so damn sweet and tender, a wave of warmth wells up inside me, and I nearly lose the ability to stand upright.

What the hell was that?

"Go," I say, and give him a shove before I fall against him and ask for another kiss just like that one. A kiss so beautiful it could make me forget that were just two people having sex.

God, I have to get my feelings under control.

I shake my head as they take off, and change into a sundress. By the time I comb out my hair and make myself a little more presentable, Quinn pulls into the driveway in her SUV. I head outside, and climb into the back with Katee and Sam, while Nina sits in the passenger seat. The cool air conditioning falls over me as I buckle up. We all make small talk as Quinn drives along the coast until we come to a quaint village I've never before explored.

She squeezes the big vehicle between two small cars, and

when we climb out, the scorching heat of the day, radiating off the black pavement, falls over me, and I damn near melt.

"Holy hot," Sam says and tugs on her T-shirt to pull it away from her body.

Katee walks ahead. "Let's get inside where there's air conditioning."

I follow them into the big store, which is full of antiques and oddly enough, smells like warm apple pie. Then I realize why. In the back there is a counter where they sell fudge and homemade goods. Jamie always did love a good apple pie. What am I saying? It didn't matter if it was apple or not. Jamie simply loves food. I make a note to grab a couple for dinner before heading out.

I find myself gravitating toward a really pretty area rug that would look great in my entrance way, but then I remember I'll be moving soon. I walk around, touch the aged side tables, dressers, and headboards, but stop when I come to a God-awful dinner gong. It makes me laugh.

"Something funny?" Nina asks as she saunters over.

I smile at her. "This is so cute. Jamie is always hungry. He's an eating machine. He's been like that for as long as I've known him. If I brought this, he'd know dinner was ready from miles away."

"Ohmigod, you have to get it," she says, and checks the price tag. "That's too funny."

"I should. He'd get a kick out of it." The thoughts of putting a smile on Jamie's face makes me grin. I love seeing him happy, love seeing the old Jamie.

"That was really nice of him to take Chase for the day. You probably haven't had a break in forever."

I nod. "He's a good uncle. He's good for Chase."

She goes a bit serious, as I examine the gong. "He seems to be doing so much better, Fallon. We were all pretty worried about him."

A niggling of guilt settles deep in my stomach. Instead of turning to Jamie in my darkest hour, I ran away. Did that hurt him? After losing his fiancée and baby, I never stopped to think that by running away he was losing me in his time of need too. How could I have been so selfish? But there is a part of me that had to run. I just couldn't be in that house, couldn't be in Seattle and around everything that reminded me of Ethan...of Sara. And what if Jamie had been able to read the worries on my face? I'm like an open book to him most times. What if he figured out what was going on inside my brain, the things I suspected were going on between my husband and his fiancée? I couldn't let him know. I would have left him gutted even more than he already was, and I couldn't be the one responsible for that. I love him too much.

"He doesn't say it, but Cole gets the sense that Jamie blames himself for the accident."

My gaze jerks to hers. "Are you kidding me? None of it was his fault. In fact..." When her eyes narrow, I let my words fall off before I say too much, say something that there's no coming back from.

"Has he ever said he thought it was his fault?" she asks, real worry in her eyes.

"No, we don't actually talk about it." But maybe, maybe in not so many words he did tell me.

I don't want you to count on me. I'll just let you down

Is it possible that he really thinks the accident was his fault?

"Why would he think that?"

"Cole's not sure. It's just a gut feeling."

"Guys, come see this," Katee says, her voice high and excited and with the way my stomach is knotting, I'm grateful for the change in conversation.

"Anyway, I'm here if you ever want to talk, okay?" Nina says, and I give her arm a grateful squeeze.

"Thanks," I say and wish I could tell her about Sara's strange phone call, but I don't want to drag her into any of this when I don't know what's going on. Katee calls again and I grab the horrendous gong and we follow her voice and find her and Sam admiring a beautiful crib.

"This is so perfect," she says.

I run my hand along the white wooden slats, and the strangest sensations go through me. It's been a long time since I thought about having more children, but all of a sudden I can't stop thinking about it. Of course, there's always artificial insemination. Then again, Jamie was excited to be a father, and is amazing with Chase so maybe he'd be onboard...

What the hell am I thinking?

"It's beautiful," I say.

"I think I'll get it and get Luke to come back later to pick it up."

"Look what I'm getting," I say and produce the gong.

"That's hilarious," Sam says. "They can use it to call us for dinner after they fry all that fish they're going to catch," she says and rolls her eyes.

We head to the cash register, and Nina helps me get a few pies, and once we pay for our goods, we make our way outside. We drop the purchases into the back of the SUV and I spot a Starbucks on the corner. "Come on, ladies. Salted caramel lattes on me."

As we head toward the corner, Katee crinkles her nose in thought and says, "I wonder if we should grab a bucket of chicken or something and take it back home. What are the odds the guys will actually catch enough, or any fish, for dinner?"

"It's a good plan," Sam says. "Ooh, look," she says and points to the swim suit store. "I could use a new suit."

"Same," Katee says, and rubs her belly. "Think they have maternity?"

"Only one way to find out," Sam says, and heads inside. I'm about to follow them, when from the corner of my eye, I catch a glimpse of a woman darting around the corner. A woman who looks an awful lot like Sara.

"Seriously," Jonah says and glances at the buckets of chicken, all the side dishes and the pies laid out on the counter. "You guys had so little faith is our hunting and gathering skills?" He raises his hand, palm up and out, displaying mock indignation as Zander and I drop the cooler onto the floor of the kitchen. Fallon looks past my shoulder and smiles. I turn to see all the kids grinning as Luke ushers them inside. I take in Daisy, who is talking a million miles an hour, her purple shirt stained with chocolate ice cream, much like the other three.

"Hunting and gathering skills, my ass," Quinn says as she plants one hand on her hip. "You had rods, and the lake was stocked."

"That makes it worse," Jonah says, incredulous. "In a stocked lake, you still didn't think we could bring home a few trout for dinner. And for the record I won. My fish was this big." He holds his hands out wide, and we all laugh as Zander pushes them closer together.

Quinn crinkles her nose. "Well, good for you, but we weren't sure if the kids would like fish. That's the only reason we got the food," she says as she winks at the other women. "Isn't that right, ladies?" she asks, and Fallon, Sam, Nina and Katee all jump in to her rescue. I smile, loving how the women took Fallon in and bonded with her. Sara was her closest friends, and as far as I know, when she left me, she left Fallon too.

"Nice try." Jonah opens the cooler to show off our catches. "For that I might not let you have any."

"Ah, good," Quinn says as she glances into the cooler at the bloody, headless fish.

"And for that, I'm going to make you eat it now," Jonah says and drags her in for a hug.

"Yuck, get away from me." She shoves him and pinches her nose. "You smell like fish."

Jonah lifts his arms and smells his shirt. "That's a good manly smell, babe."

"Come on, let's go dunk you in the ocean before you shower. I don't even want you inside the cottage smelling like this."

"I want to swim, too!" Chase exclaims.

"I know I need to dunk," I say.

"Let's all hit the beach before dinner," Fallon says.

"Oh, by the way," Zander says to Sam. "I hope you're up for a sleepover. Daisy invited the kids over."

Sam throws her hands up in the air. "The more the merrier." I don't miss the stiffness in Fallon's spine. Sam must notice it too, because she turns to the women and says, "That's if you're all okay with it, of course."

"Like you have to twist my arm," Quinn responds with a snort. "Scotty is all yours."

"I'm sure Brandon would love that," Nina says.

Fallon crosses her arms. "I'm...not sure."

"Can I, Mommy, can I?" Chase pleads, his brown eyes big and begging.

Quinn snorts. "I'm telling you know, that boy is going to be a heartbreaker when he grows up." She laughs as his long thick lashes fall slowly over dark chocolate eyes. "Oh, you are in for so much trouble."

I step up to Fallon. "They're only three houses down. I think Chase would love it." I lean in to her, and lower my voice for her ears only. "I spent the day thinking about all the ways I can make you scream my name tonight, and now you won't have to worry about little ears hearing it."

She swallows, and I love the soft pink color creeping into her cheeks. "When you put it that way." She glances at Sam. "It's okay by me, but he's not used to sleepovers. So…"

"If he cries to come home, Zander will bring him, but I think little mother hen over there," she says, pointing to Daisy, who is doting on Scotty, "Is going to make sure he has fun."

"It's settled. Let's get the stink off these guys," Katee says.

"I'll get my water wings," Chase says and runs from the kitchen.

As everyone files out the door, Fallon reaches into a bag and pulls out a new bathing suit.

I take the material and run it though my hands. "What's this?" I ask.

"New suit."

I frown at the polka dot two-piece. "But I liked your old one. I liked it a lot."

She goes up on her toes, and puts her mouth near my ear, "Well, you can't very well be hanging out on the beach with a perma-boner, now can you?"

A groan born from sexual need rises in my throat. "And you think this is going to change that? One look at your beautiful body in this and I'm a goner."

The smile that comes over her face fucks me over, and it's all I can do not to drag her into my arms and take her right here on the counter. But tonight, however. Tonight, I'm going to have her here all to myself and I plan to take full advantage of it. Oh, yeah, I want this woman at my mercy while I do dirty things to her.

"Great, now I'm going to have to whack off before going for a swim," I say and her laughter trails behind her as she dashes upstairs. I tug off my shirt and toss it into the washing machine, and grab a bottle of water from the fridge. I crack it open and take a drink, needing something to cool me down.

Fallon comes back down with Chase, and one look at her and I begin to thicken. After last night, you'd think I'd be sated, but no, the more time I spend with her, the more I want her—in so many ways. And that's all kinds of fucked up.

"You like?" she asks when she reaches the landing.

I growl, and put my hand on her curvy hip when Chase runs past us. "I'm going to wreck you tonight," I say and hand her the bottle of water. She wraps her lips around it and takes a long pull. When she finishes, she wipes her mouth with the back of her hand, and her chest heaves.

"Promise?" she asks with a sexy grin that wraps around my cock and tugs.

"Let's go, Jamie," Chase says from the door.

"Hey, what about me? she asks, with a laugh. "Jeez, you spend one day fishing with him, and he forgets all about me."

"I didn't forget about you," I assure her. "And I promise to show you that later." I put my hand on her back and urge her to go ahead of me, partly because Chase is jumping up and down and eager to go, and partly because I want to see her ass in those cute bikini bottoms. She opens the door, and takes Chase's hand when he looks like he's about to dart away without us.

"Mommy, Huxley was chasing the fish today."

"Was he really?" she asks.

"Can we get a Huxley?"

"We can talk about that," she says, and before I reach her, her cell phone rings. She goes perfectly still, her body as stiff as a surfboard.

"What?" I ask.

Her eyes widen. Why does she look so spooked?

"Nothing. Just leave it," she says lightly, but her body language is telling a different story. Who does she think is calling, and why does she not want to answer?

"Are you sure?" I jerk my thumb over my shoulder. "I can grab it for you?"

She nods quickly. "It's vacation time. No electronics," she says. "And I don't think Chase can wait another minute."

"Fair enough."

Chase tugs on her hand. "Come on, Mommy."

Forgetting her ringing phone, I step outside with them, and shut the door behind us. The late day sun falls over Fallon, lighting a halo over her head. Her flip flops smack against her feet as she hurries down the beach toward the water. Huxley comes running when he sees Chase, and it doesn't surprise me. It was love at first sight for Chase, and he spent more time playing with the dog than fishing today. Worms really aren't his thing, and that thought makes me chuckle. No, dogs are definitely his thing and I'm glad Fallon is considering one. Ethan wasn't a lover of dogs, having been bit as a child in the park. To be fair, it was an incredibly hot day, and he'd been teasing the dog with a stick, no matter how many times I told him to stop. The animal nipped his ear in protest, and he'd disliked dogs ever since.

Fallon kicks her flip flops off and goes from one foot to the other. "The sand is smoking hot," she says as her lush breasts bounce with the movement. I stare, mesmerized.

Motherfucker.

Is she trying to kill me?

"That's not the only thing that's hot," I whisper into her ear as I scoop her up.

"Don't you dare dunk me again," she says as her hands circle my neck to hold on.

"Just saving your feet from the hot sand." As a burst of happiness fills the gaping hole in my soul, and before I realize what I'm doing, I give her a kiss on the cheek.

Chase laughs. "You kissed Mommy. You kissed Mommy," he says and rolls on the sand with Huxley.

"Come on, Chase," Quinn says laughing. "Let's get Huxley cooled off in the water."

Huxley runs out and Chase goes after him. Fallon is about to jump from my arms to follow them in, but I hold her tight. "It's okay. Quinn's got him," I assure her.

"I'm just not used to other people caring for him."

"You've done a lot on your own for a very long time," I say, and that's when I realize how alone she's been, even before she lost her husband. Ethan was on the road a lot, maybe more than he needed to be. No wonder they were having trouble in their marriage.

"I'm used to taking care of everything myself," she says, and my gut clenches. Goddammit, I want to be the guy she can count on, the guy that takes care of her inside the bedroom and out. But what if I let her down again? What if I can't be the man she needs? Being here on the ocean it's easy to forget real life exists, but it does, and when we get back home, things have to go back to normal.

Right?

"Jamie?" she asks.

As my heart swells with the things I feel for her I walk into the water. "Tonight I'm totally going to take care of you," I say and set her on her feet. She gives me a quizzical look.

"Is everything okay?"

I slide my hand around her head, and bring her lips to

mine for a kiss. I suddenly don't even care who's watching. I break the kiss and Chase comes running over, splashing us both.

"Chase," Fallon yelps and hugs herself in the chilly ocean water. She scoops up her son and he laughs as she spins him. The dog starts barking and running circles around us, and I can't keep the smile from my face.

"Who wants to play Frisbee?" Luke calls from the sand.

"Hey, Chase, you want to play?"

"Frisbee," he calls out and Fallon sets him down.

I take a fast dunk to get the smell off fish off my body, and the women lay out their towels as we form a circle with the kids and start playing frisbee. All four kids are pretty athletic, not a surprise considering their parents. Watching Chase does make me want to get him in a pair of skates, though.

We play for a solid hour as the women sunbathe, and when I hear a bunch of rumbling stomachs—okay, it might have just been mine—I stop the game. "Who wants to fry up some fish?" I ask, and Daisy pulls a face of disgust that makes us all laugh.

"I guess it's a good thing the girls bought that chicken," Jonah says.

"Told you so," Quinn calls out.

"She doesn't miss a thing," Jonah says and shakes his head. "Now I'll be paying for this all night." He calls for Huxley who is nipping at the waves. "Let's all head back to my place. I know I caught the biggest fish, but since I'm the best cook..."

Moans and groans of disbelief come from the others, and as I laugh, and as everyone makes their way back to the cottages, Chase tugs my hand. His brow is furrowed, and worried something is wrong, I drop to my knees. "What's up, bud?"

"Can you be my daddy?" he asks, and my damn heart leaps

into my throat. Damn, he's a smart boy, and I never should have kissed Fallon in front of him. What the hell was I thinking? I wasn't, and that's the problem. Being with Fallon makes me forget about life for a while, and why I can't be with her.

"Chase," I begin and glance at the clouds moving across the blue sky. "Your daddy is up there watching over you remember?"

"But I want a daddy here," he says and jumps up and down in the sand. "Everyone has their daddy here. Why don't I?"

Because of me.

The others move away to give us our privacy, and I cast a glance to my left to find Fallon staring at us, perfectly still, her jaw open, every muscle in her body pulled tight. Christ, I'm not even sure she's breathing. Then again, I'm having a hell of a time filling my constricted lungs. I swallow the massive amount of guilt pushing bile into my throat, and struggle to find the right words to help Chase understand the situation.

"I can do things with you," I say to appease him and when he looks like he's about to cry, I quickly add, "Like a daddy would." Oh, fuck I think I might have just made this worse.

I give Fallon a pleading look that sets her in to motion. She steps up to me and I stand. "He's hungry and tired," she says quietly, for my ears only. "That's when all this gets the best of him."

"I want to play hockey like you," he says, switching subjects so fast I'm sure it must have given him whiplash.

"Yeah, I can take you to the rink. Teach you how to play. Would you like that, Chase?" I ask as my heart crashes against my chest. I swallow and my throat aches. "I can do things like that with you."

He smiles up at me. "Like a daddy," he says, as if it's all settled.

I glance at Fallon. How the hell do I answer that? I don't

want to agree, and give him the wrong expectations, but how can I disagree when all he wants is for me to be like a daddy.

"How about we go get something to eat and drink?" Fallon says and ruffles his hair.

"I want to cook the fish," he says and takes my hand and tugs me along. I look over my shoulder and even though Fallon had been playing it cool, I catch the stricken look on her face.

"I'm sure Jonah will want your help," I say to him. "Once he knows how good you are at making pancakes."

Fallon is exceptionally quiet when we reach the house, and while the guys gather up the cooler, and the women take the food to Johan's place—giving me a shaky smile as they go—I run upstairs for a fast shower. While I do want to get cleaned up, I need a moment of reprieve. I take a few deep breaths, and work to get myself together as my pulse continues to pounds against my neck.

Fallon said she had no interested in dating again, but goddammit if Chase doesn't need—deserve—a father. But Fallon said marriage wasn't in her future. But she deserves to have a man in her life, someone who makes her happy and could be a good influence for her son.

Fuck if it isn't a role I want.

The shower door inches open and I blink to find Fallon standing there, now dressed in a light sundress with spaghetti straps. "Hey," she says quietly, cautiously. "You okay?"

"Yeah, good. You?"

"Sorry about that earlier. I think he just sees the other kids with their dad and he's young and doesn't really understand."

"Yeah, I get it," I say. She opens her mouth like she wants to say more, then her gaze scans the length of me.

"If only we didn't have somewhere to be," she says playfully, and I get she's trying to lighten the mood around us.

"Tonight I plan to tie you up and have my way with you all night long," I inform her and she sucks her bottom lip into her mouth. I dip my head, study her lush lips, lips I'd love to feel wrapped around my hard cock. "You like that idea, I take it."

"Maybe I'll tie you up," she says as she turns around, giving a saucy shake of her sweet ass as she turns to go.

"You keep shaking that ass of yours at me…" I warn, my voice dropping an octave.

"What?" she asks and coils her fingers in her hair as she turns to me, eager to hear what I have to say

"I might just fuck it," I say bluntly, and her eyes go saucer-wide.

Sweet Jesus, she's never had anal sex before.

"You've got a dirty little mouth on you, Jamie Adams," she says as she quivers beneath my heated gaze.

I grab a towel from the hook, and start drying my body. "A dirty mouth you want between your legs, you mean," I say.

"Yeah," she says breathlessly like her thoughts are a million miles away. Perhaps she's visualizing the last time I buried my face in her sweet pussy. "Oh," she says blinking her eyes back into focus. "About that fishing trip and you taking Chase. I'm not sure I ever thanked you for that," she teases.

"You can, tonight. You can thank me all over, baby," I say and run the towel over my throbbing cock.

She wets her lips. "We better go," she says breathlessly. "The others will wonder what's taking us so long."

"I think they could all figure it out pretty quickly," I say with a chuckle.

She laughs, and her footsteps echo in the hall and reach my ears as she heads down the stairs. I dart to my room, and from the first floor, Fallon's cell phone rings. It keeps ringing and ringing and I'm not so sure she's going to answer it.

I tug on a shirt, and a pair of shorts and hurry downstairs.

Chase is gone, and I can only assume he left with the others. I step into the kitchen and listen to the one-way conversation. Fallon is nodding her head and agreeing to whatever the person on the other end is saying.

She finally disconnects and glances at me. "That was the realtor. We've had two showings already and he has some places lined up for me to look at when we get back."

I nod. "I'll go with you. Make sure the places are sound."

She drops her phone on the counter, leaving it here, and picks up Chase's backpack and says, "We'd better go." I turn and nearly have a heart attack when I hear a big booming sound. "What the hell?" The house practically vibrates. "Are we having an earthquake?"

"No. Come on," she says and from the way she's trying to hide a chuckle I get she's up to something. She ushers me out the door and we go to Jonah's place, find everyone gathered around the fire pit as Jonah fries the fish. My gaze goes to a big gong.

"What is that thing?" I ask.

"It's a dinner gong," Fallon says. "I picked it up today." She leans into me and laughs. "I know how you hate to miss a meal and now you'll know when dinner is ready."

"That is not coming home with us," I say, and instantly realize I used the word *us*.

"Oh, it's definitely coming home with us," Fallon says.

Home.

Fuck, the thoughts of making a home with Fallon and Chase...

"Not happening," I say, and she just gives me a grin, because I think she knows, no matter what, I'll give in and always give her what she wants.

Is it possible that she could want more from me?

"That stinks," Daisy says, and we all laugh as she plugs her nose and points to the fish cooking over the fire.

"And that is why we bought chicken," Quinn says. "Come on kids, let's go find something yummy to eat."

Fallon stands and takes Chase inside to make him up a plate, and I stare at her ass as I watch her go.

"Beer?" Cole asks and hands me a bottle.

I take a long pull and relax into my lawn chair, waiting for a lecture from him that doesn't come, thank God.

But when he plunks himself down beside me, he does say, "The Johnsons' property is going up for sale. I was talking to Fred the other day. His wife put her hip out and the house is too much upkeep for them."

"Oh yeah," I say. "Sorry to hear about her hip."

"If you're still interested in a property."

I angle my head, look down the stretch of beach, take in the Johnsons' property on the cove. It's a nice place, but I have no reason to buy a cottage anymore, although it would be a good investment. Properties out here only go up in value.

"Good investment," Cole says, like he can read my mind.

"True."

"Plus, Fallon and Chase seem to love it here."

"Yeah, they do," I say.

"Did I just hear my name," Fallon says as she comes back out with Chase, who is chomping down on a chicken leg.

"I was just telling Jamie here the Johnsons' are selling their cottage. The one on the cove over there," he says pointing.

She glances out into the distance. "It's beautiful. Are you thinking of buying it?" she asks.

I open my mouth, about to say no, when Cole says, "I can get you a tour tomorrow."

"I bet it's gorgeous and perfect for you," Fallon says and Cole smirks at me. Why the fuck is he pushing this? I told him Fallon and I weren't a couple. We're just having sex. Amazing sex. The best sex of my life.

Fuck, I'm screwed.

Soon enough, we're all seated around the fire, eating dinner and then roasting marshmallows. Fallon looks happy and relaxed and my heart beats a little faster when I hear her laugh. Day bleeds to night as the sun sets on the horizon, and soon enough the little ones are all rubbing their eyes.

Fallon calls Chase over, says something to him about the sleepover, and he nods. Zander and Sam gather up the kids, and we all say goodnight. Fallon comes and sits next to me. I hand her my beer and she takes a drink.

"Want to go for a swim, or walk on the beach?" I ask even though I'm eager to get her alone.

"Maybe later," she says with a coy smile. "Right now I want to go back to the cottage." She stands and gives a teasing shake to her ass as she walks away.

Oh yeah, she wants it, and damned if I'm not going to give it to her.

FALLON

As soon as I walk through the front door, Jamie grabs me, and in a move that has need written all over it, he pushes my chest to the wall and pins my hands over my head.

"Just like that," he says. "Don't you dare move. Tonight, you're all mine, and I'm going to make you fucking scream."

My chest heaves and I breathe hard, loving the way he's taking charge of my body and our play. I widen my fingers on the wall as his hands slide down my arms, shape my curves and massage my outer thighs. He pushes against me, and his cock is already hard and eager. To know I can do this to him without even touching his body thrills me and fills me with a new kind of freedom.

I whimper loudly at the sound of the door closing and the bolt sliding home as Jamie locks the world out and us in. I don't believe I've ever wanted anyone quite the way I want this man. It's exciting and scary and different, and instead of thinking too hard on it, I'm just going to go with it. But as he puts his hands on my backside and squeezes, it does make me wonder if he's really going to follow through with the threat and take me in a way I've never been taken before..

My heart picks up tempo. I've never been taking like that before, and at the heart of the matter it's like this—I want to be taken like that, but not by anyone. I want it to be Jamie. Not only would I never trust a man with my body like that, I want him to be my first. He slides his hands around me, and takes a fistful of my breasts.

"I need to fuck these," he says. "Seeing you in that fucking bathing suit today." He nips at my shoulder and growls. "All I could think about was sliding my cock between these beautiful tits, riding you hard and coming in your mouth."

"Jamie," I say. "I want that."

"But then this," he says, pushing his cock against my ass. "So lush and so sexy and when you shake it at me, it fucks me over."

"Do you mean like this?" I move against his erection.

He growls loudly into my ear. "You want me to fuck your virgin ass, Fallon?" he asks, his voice a low gravelly whisper.

"Yes," I murmur.

"You sure about that?" he asks as he lifts my sundress, exposing my lace panties. "I might lose my mind and wreck this pretty ass of yours."

"Wreck me," I say, even though I know he won't. No, Jamie is going to take good care of me, that I know. "Take me. Do anything, everything, with me," letting him know he's not alone in this insanity between us. This pull, need—intense hunger—that's always been there, but kept on a tight leash.

Until now.

He spins me around and I catch the intensity in his gaze as his mouth closes over mine. He kisses me hard, deeply, until I'm practically a puddle at his feet. He slides a hand around me and lifts me onto his hips. I link my hands behind his head and move restlessly against his beautiful, fat cock.

"Mine," he says as he carries me down the hall and into the kitchen.

"Bedroom too far," he murmurs, and sets me on the counter. "Need you naked. Now." His face is eye level with my breasts and in one fast move he grips the fabric and rips open my dress. I gasp as the buttons scatter to the floor and honest to God, I've never seen Jamie so crazed before.

I love it.

He tugs down my bra, and takes my nipple into his mouth as he tweaks my other one with his fingers. I flatten my hands on the island counter behind me, and lean back, sticking my full chest out even more, offering up everything to this man. It might be emotional suicide. Heck, I know it is. But I'm his. I've always been his, whether he wants all of me or not.

"Just like that," he says and his growl of approval brings a smile to my face. Jamie unleashed is a thing of beauty. He bites down on my nipple, then lick it, turning beautiful pain into glorious pleasure.

"Lift," he says and smacks my thigh. Bracing my hands, I lift my ass, and he grips my panties and slides them down my legs. He brings them to his nose and inhales. "I fucking love the smell of you." He shoves my panties into his back pocket and his fingers dig into my thighs to widen me more.

He steps back, lets his gaze rake over me. His pink tongue slides out and he wets his lips, looking at me like I'm a buffet and he's going to sample one of everything. Twice.

Yes, please...

"Remove the dress," he commands in a soft voice. I grip what's left of the ripped fabric and slide it off my shoulders. "So fucking nice," he says, his gaze latched on my breasts spilling out from my bra. I reach around and unhook it, and toss it to the floor with the rest of the clothes.

As I sit there completely naked, his to do with as he pleases, he scrubs his face and his gaze meets mine. "Lay back, baby." The softness in his voice pulls a whimper from my throat.

I fall back onto the island, and the coolness of the marble chills my flesh, but the second he positions himself between my spread legs, and puts his mouth on my clit, my temperature jumps a few degrees.

"Jamie," I murmur.

"Louder," he says from between my legs.

I call his name louder and as my voice fills the air, he rewards me by sliding a finger into my sex. My muscles ripple, and I just about come.

"Easy, baby," he says. "I want to play with you for a bit." He toys with me, lightly touching the bundle of nerves inside me, as he laps at my clit. Then he pulls his mouth away, and his fat finger stills inside me.

He's not doing anything to me, not stroking, not teasing. The only thing going on is his finger filling me, and I don't think I've ever been so freaking turned on in my life.

"Jamie, what are you doing to me?" I ask, and toss my head from side to side.

"Nothing, baby. I'm not doing a damn thing."

"Then why am I so close to coming?"

His chuckle curls around me. "You like having my finger in you, doing nothing at all."

"It's not doing nothing. It's doing everything."

"If I move it, you're going to come, baby."

I go up on my elbows to catch his devilish smile and begin panting. "Jamie. Oh my God, I can't even believe what's going on with my body right now." I begin moving my hips, riding his finger, encouraging him to move, and while I like him finger fucking me, I swear this comes with its own pleasure that's completely twisting me up inside.

"You can ride my finger if you want," he says, but he's not as in control as he's letting on. There's a needy hitch to his voice and he's hanging on by a thread. But watching me work my pussy over his finger might just be the blade that cuts it.

I buck against him, and he growls. "I love when you take what you want," he says. I pound against his hand, and he looks at my breasts. "Yeah, after licking all your cum clean, I'm going to get my cock in there," he says, and his dirty words push me closer and closer to the edge.

His thumb swipes my clit. "Oh. My. Yes," I cry out. "Please, Jamie, put your mouth on me."

"That what you need, baby?"

"Yes!"

"Fine, lay back. Don't move. Stay completely still for me."

The heat in his eyes tells me he wants me at his mercy. I want that too, so I fall back, and place my hands at my sides as he puts his mouth on me again, his tongue circling my clit, coming close but never touching. I'm about ready to burst from sexual frustration, but it's good, so goddamn good.

I fist my hands, and my nails dig into my palms. "Please, please, please," I beg and he chuckles against my sex. The vibrations go through me, turn me on even more. He pushes another finger into me, and ever so slowly starts fucking my pussy. I'm so wet and slick, he easily slides in and out. I move my hips, and he pulls his mouth off me.

"No moving," he says, and I go still.

He returns to eating me, and inside me, his fingers pick up the pace, and while moving is fun, staying still and letting him take control comes with its own torturous excitement. He finally—finally—licks my clit, and small tremors begin in my core. His fingers move faster, hard blunt strokes meant to take me where I need to go.

I concentrate on the pleasure welling up inside me, the slide of his tongue, and the way he sweeps his fingers over the bundle of nerves inside me—the prefect trifecta.

I claw at the counter as heat bursts inside me, and his

deep needy growl as I come all over his fingers increases the intensity between my legs. Sex has never, ever, been this good for me before. How will I ever go back to my bland, boring sex life after this?

Jamie lightly licks me, and pets my sex softly as he slowly brings me back down. When the room comes back into view again, I go up on my elbows.

"How do you do that?" I ask.

"Do what?"

"Make me come so hard."

"You should always come like that, Fallon."

"My vibrator should be hanging its head in shame," I say, and he laughs at my brutal honesty.

"My hand does the job for me," he informs me. "But that's just for release. Watching you come undone. That's makes all my orgasms better." He shakes his head, and gazes the length of me. "Your body. It's a fucking shrine worthy of worship."

The way this man adores my body, takes pleasure in burying himself between my legs...I just can't even. "I want you, Jamie. I want you in my mouth. I want you *everywhere*..." I say, unashamed of my needs.

"This sweet ass of yours, baby. We'll get there, but not tonight." He puts his finger into my mouth and I suck. "Yeah, tonight, that's where my cock wants to be."

He scoops me up from the island, and carries me upstairs and sets me on the bed. "I get to spend the whole night in here with you," he says, looking at me like an excited kid who got the pony he always wanted for Christmas. My heart misses a beat...then another.

"Jamie..."

"Lay back for me, babe," he murmurs. I position myself and his knees dig into the bed as he straddles my body. "Widen your mouth."

I put two pillows behind my head to better position

myself for what he wants, and I part my lips. He growls. "Damn, that mouth," he says and grunts as he takes his hard cock into his hand. He squeezes and come drips from the slit. He rubs it between my breasts to lubricate my skin, and when he gets me all nice and wet, I cup my breasts, squeeze them together for him.

"Oh, baby, yeah, just like that," he says and pinches my swollen nipple. He shimmies higher, and pushes his thick cock between my swollen and achy breasts, and when he powers forward, I capture his crown in my mouth.

"Hot as fuck,' he whispers, and leans over my body to grip the headboard. I massage my breasts, rubbing his cock between them as he moves his hips, fucking my tits and mouth at the same time. It's absolutely glorious.

"You feel so damn good," he says, and I lick him, eager for his cum. He fucks me harder, powers into my mouth, and his growls fill the quiet of the room. His grunts tell me he's close, but holding off, wanting to prolong the pleasure. His cock goes a little deeper into my mouth, and I widen my lips to accommodate his girth.

I moan with pleasure, and when he pulls back, I whisper, "I love the taste of you."

"You want my cum?" he grunts out.

"Mmm," is all I can manage to mutter as his cock hits the back of my throat. His body tenses, and his muscles flex as he strokes, once, twice, and positions his cock right over my open mouth. I take a fast breath and a second later, cum spills from his slit and onto my tongue. I let my breasts go, and cup his ass as I take all he's offering. I savor his taste on my tongue before swallowing. Groaning and grunting, he depletes himself, and his ass relaxes in my hands.

He lifts one leg, and goes down on his back beside me. "Come here," he says, and pulls me to him. I give a contented sigh, my muscles weak and fatigued.

"So you have a vibrator," he says, his voice teasing and playful.

Chuckling, I say, "I do tend to spill secrets when I'm in bed with you."

He takes my hand and brings it to his mouth, to kiss it softly and my heart fills with the things I feel for him. He angles his head, checks the clock.

"It's early. Want to walk along the beach?"

"As long as you don't toss me into the water."

"Would I do that?" he asks, feigning innocence.

"Yeah, you would."

"Okay, I would. But I like you when you're all wet," he murmurs, and as he gazes at me, hunger once again dances in his eyes. He flips me over, places a pillow beneath my hips and as he kneads my ass, plays with my opening, I'm pretty sure it will be a while before we actually take that walk.

12

JAMIE

I glance at the beautiful woman in my arms, her head resting on my chest. It's nearing midnight, but I don't want to go to sleep. No, I want to enjoy every moment with Fallon before we have to go back to the real world.

"Interested in that walk?" I ask her.

She stretches and in a soft voice murmurs, "As long as you promise not to dunk me."

"I promise," I say and drop a soft kiss onto her head. "Let's go."

We both slide from the bed, dress and a few minutes later we step out into the dark night. On the beach I catch a few couples walking in the moonlight. Waves lap gently against the shore, and the sound soothes my soul. Fallon's flip flops snap against her heels as we walk and when we reach the water, she takes them off.

She squeezes the sand between her toes. "Much cooler than this afternoon," she says.

"Yeah, but you're still hot," I say and glance at her frayed shorts and snug t-shirt.

"Food and sex. Are those the only things you think about?" she teases.

"Hockey, don't forget hockey," I say.

"Right."

As the moonlight falls over us, and it's just the two of us on the beach now, I capture her hand. She glances up at me, and gives me a small smile.

"It feels weird not having Chase with me."

"It's okay to have some time for yourself, Fallon. It's been a rough year."

"For all of us," she says and gives my hand a little squeeze.

We've only been here a couple of days, but already she seems like a different person. We walk for a long time, until we reach the cove where the cottage is for sale. As I take in the quaint place with the white fence, and matching shutters, I suddenly picture myself in the yard with Chase, playing ball, or shooting pucks in a net, knowing later that night I'd be falling in to bed with the woman I love. In a perfect world, that's how my life would have played out.

"What do you want, Fallon?" I ask.

"What do you mean?" she asks.

"In a perfect world, what would you want?"

"Well you know me, I'm a simple girl from Spokane, and I never needed much to make me happy."

"I always liked that about you." The wind pushes a lock of honey blonde hair across her face, and I touch her cheek, slide it behind her ear. "You were different like that."

"I didn't come from a lot, so material things aren't that big to me. I'm more about family, relationships, integrity...*loyalty*." I note the way she emphasizes the word loyal. Was Ethan not loyal to her? "But I have to say, I sure could get used to having a place like this on the ocean," she teases as she looks at the cottage on the cove.

"Sara and I were going to..."

"I know." She swallows, her eyes big and a bit haunted. "Have you...heard anything from Sara after she left?" she asks.

"No, nothing. She just took off. She hates me, and I don't blame her."

She stops and turns to me, her eyes narrow, worry on her face. "Why do you think she hates you?"

I scoff. "I was supposed to take her to her appointment that day. I was the one who was supposed to be driving, not Ethan. If practice hadn't run late and I had made it home on time, maybe none of this would have happened. I'm to blame for everything."

"Wait, you think they were on their way to some appointment?" she asks, incredulous, like I'm wrong about that.

Why would I be wrong? I briefly pinch my eyes shut, and rewind to the week before the accident. Sara had told me she had a doctor's appointment the next week. I remember I was texting with Ethan, and was only half listening. But after the accident I apologized a million times for not being the one to drive her to her appointment. She never said she wasn't on her way to one, and agreed that I was to blame for everything.

"Yeah, she had a doctor's appointment."

Fallon starts walking again. "Are you one hundred percent sure?"

I touch her arm to stop her. "What are you getting at?"

She looks ahead, her lashes low, shadowing her eyes. "Nothing. I just didn't know she had an appointment. She usually told me those things." She starts walking again, and I keep pace beside her. She goes quiet, and after a long while she says, "It wasn't your fault, Jamie. You can't ever think that."

"Why not?"

"You just can't," she says and once again I get the sinking sensation that she's keeping something from me.

"Have you heard from Sara?" I ask, and when her body tightens, I have my answer. "Why didn't you tell me?" *This* is what she's been keeping private?

"Actually, I wasn't sure I should. I didn't want to ruin your vacation here. You seem happier, Jamie. More like the old you and I like being with that guy."

"What did she want?" I ask. It's not like Fallon to keep things from me. She knows I hate secrets and value trust.

"She asked if I was with you. I posted a picture on Instagram, and she must have recognized the beach."

I look out over the water, my stomach clenching hard. "She liked it here."

"Then I...I thought I saw her, but that's crazy. She couldn't be here, right? I mean, why would she be?"

My heart crashes a little harder as I glance around. "You think she's here?"

"I don't know." She gives a non-committal shrug. "If she is, wouldn't she have reached out to you?"

"I'm not so sure about that." A wave comes up and I jump back to avoid it. "It is possible she's vacationing around here. She loved this area."

"Do you know where she went when she left?"

I glance up when off in the distance I hear music coming from an open window. Sound really travels here, so I lower my voice. "Probably back to San Diego. That's where her parents live."

"That makes sense." A beat of silence and then, "Do you... ever think..." she crinkles her nose, like she can't bring herself to ask.

"What, that we'll get back together?"

"Yes."

"She hates me, Fallon." A tortured noise catches in my throat. "I'm pretty sure a reunion is never going to happen."

"What if she doesn't hate you?" she asks quietly, and looks down like she's remembering something.

"She does. End of story." I swallow the lump in my throat and turn things back to her. "Would finding the perfect man for you and Chase be part of your perfect world?" I ask, redirecting the conversation.

She gives a fast shake of her head. "I don't want to date again. I can't go through that, but yes, when it comes right down to it, I would like Chase to have a father."

"And you, Fallon? Do you want a husband? Would that make you happy?"

"Yes," she says quietly. "But he'd have to be kind, loyal, loving, and put the needs of his family first."

"I didn't put Sara's needs first and that's why she was in the car accident."

"No, Jamie. You always put the needs of others first. Always. Believe me, I know," she says quietly, then she opens her mouth like she wants to say more, but closes it again.

"You deserve that kind of happiness, you know. You deserve a guy like that."

Goddammit, if I don't want to be that guy for her.

"Thanks. You do too, Jamie."

I shake my head. "No, I don't."

"Life goes on whether we want it too or not. It's time for us both to move on with it." She gives me a wobbly smile. "Actually, I change my answer."

I give her a perplexed frown.

"You know what would make me happy, Jamie." I stare at her, wait for her to continue. She pokes me in the chest, and I capture her hand. Her other hand goes to my face, a soft caress that soothes my tormented soul. Need blows through me like a summer storm. Fuck, I missed her. Missed us. "For you to be happy," she whispers, her breath shuddering against my skin.

"The accident wasn't your fault, and never once did I think it was. You need to let go of the guilt. You are the best guy I know. The best guy I've ever known. No one blames you."

"Sara blames me. She wouldn't have left otherwise."

"Not true. I never blamed you and I left. Maybe she just has some things to work out in her head."

"Fallon," I begin quietly as loss and sorrow squeeze my heart.

"Yeah."

"You left. You...didn't turn to me. I thought...thought you blamed me. You always used to turn to me."

She wraps her arms around me and holds me close, loosening the knot of tension between my shoulder blades, and calming the heavy thud of my heart. "Oh, Jamie, no. Believe me, the accident was not your fault. Please tell me you believe me."

"But I wasn't—"

"No, Jamie. Stop." A small shaky breath passes her lips as she shuts down my argument. "You need to stop. You need to just trust me, okay?"

"I do trust you, Fallon. Trust is one of the most important things to me. You know that, right?"

"I do, and I would never ask for it, if I wasn't sure the accident had nothing to do with you." She pounds softly against my chest, tears brimming in her eyes.

"Okay," I say quietly, some of the tightness in my chest ebbing away as a small measure of guilt lifts from my shoulders.

She never left because she blamed me.

Beneath the moonlight, we hold on to one another like our lives depend on it, and somehow I think it does. She sniffles against my shirt, and lifts her gaze to mine. Streaks of yellow, marbled in her pretty blue eyes, sparkles in the moonlight as the connection between us, the need, becomes emotionally charged.

"In a perfect world, what would make you happy?" she asks as I rest my forehead against hers.

Damned if that isn't a loaded question.

"To turn back time," is all I say, and she nods as I put my arm around her and start walking along the shore again. Yeah, if I could I'd go back to many years ago, and make Fallon my girl before Ethan had the chance. But that's a selfish thought because Ethan isn't here, and Sara and I lost our unborn baby, and life just isn't fucking fair.

But does that mean I can't have what I really want, can't move forward...can't find a new normal. I pull Fallon close. Every fiber of my being tells me there's more between us than sex. I can't change the past, and I'm not sure I can ever fully forgive myself. But after being with Fallon—her belief in me filling that hollowed-out spot in my chest, and lightening the heaviness in my heart—I don't think I can *live* in that past any longer either. Maybe we can somehow find our normal together and I can be the man she needs, the father Chase needs. Maybe she's right. Maybe Cole is, too.

Maybe I do deserve happiness.

As I pack things up, our glorious week at the beach over tomorrow, I think back to my conversation with Jamie that night we walked along the shore. We talked about what our lives would be like in a perfect world. I love my son more than life itself, but my life with Ethan was far from perfect, and crumbling more with each passing day.

Jamie told me if he could, he'd turn back time. I can only imagine he meant he'd go back to before the accident, when Ethan was here, when Sara and his unborn baby were living in his house. That was his perfect, obviously. A place where grief and guilt didn't weigh on him heavily. But it wouldn't have been perfect for long. Once the baby was born, I'm pretty certain we all would have had lost anyway. My mind rewinds to my phone conversation with Sara. She'd told me she loved *him*. But *him* might have meant Ethan, not Jamie. And the baby she was carrying, well…

Trust is so important to Jamie and I wanted to tell him my suspicions. Lord knows he can't keep blaming himself for an accident that wasn't his fault, but I don't want to hurt him—it would shatter him to learn my husband and his fiancée were having an affair— a woman knows these things. But I need to have the proof—which undoubtedly exists on Ethan's phone—before I do or say anything. But what if Sara shows up and wants him back? Will he want her back too? If he does, what do I do? Tell him what I think, or keep my mouth quiet? How could I let my best friend, the man I've loved for many years now, go back to a woman who was carrying a baby that likely wasn't his? I wrack my brain and as my stomach cramps, I work to clear my thoughts, leaving them to mull over later, when we're back home.

This is our last night in the gorgeous oceanside cottage, and with Chase sleeping over with the other kids at Nina and Cole's, I plan to have Jamie all to myself in that king-sized bed. I plan to give him a part of me I've never given another, and hope that on some level, he realizes he *is* the man for me —that we belong together. I spent years hiding what I felt and I can't do it any more, not after this incredible week in his arms. I can't pretend this is just sex when it's so much more. Yes, I'm risking losing my best friend if I'm mistaken about his feelings, but I'm taking a chance that when we leave here, we can be so much more. Jamie just needs to open up, and take a risk on us.

With Jamie getting Chase settled in for his overnight sleepover, and taking an awfully long time doing it, I finish packing, jump in the shower, and grin as I think about the plan I schemed up today. I rinse the rest of the sand and salty water from my sun-kissed skin, dry off with a big fluffy towel and pull on a sexy little camisole and underwear set that I picked up that day I got the bathing suit. I've been saving it for a special night—and this is it.

I give myself a once over in the mirror, and as I look at my curves, I find beauty in them—thanks to Jamie. I take in the soft pink glow on my cheeks. It's not from the sun, it's from blossoming under Jamie's touch.

The downstairs door opens, and Jamie calls out to me. Instead of answering, I rush to the dinner gong and hit it. As the sound vibrates through the house, I spread myself across the bed and wait for Jamie to find me. His footsteps pound on the stairs, and I chuckle silently at his eagerness.

"Fallon?" he calls out. "Where are you?"

I keep quiet as he rounds the corner and finds me sprawled out for him. A wide smile splits his lip. "I change my mind on the dinner gong. It's definitely coming home with us."

A home with Jamie. It's all I ever wanted.

He tugs his shirt off as he enters the room. "Like you said, sex and food, it's all I ever think about and now I get to bury my mouth between your legs and eat all night long. This is perfect, Fallon. You're perfect," he says, and a fine quiver goes through me. His nostrils flare as he comes close. He touches my lacy camisole, rubs it gently between his fingers.

"This is new."

"You like?"

"I hope you didn't pay a lot for it."

I sit up, a little worried. "You don't like it?"

In a move that catches me by surprise, he pulls me to my feet, and my body collides with his. "Oh, you've got it all wrong, babe," he growls his voice dropping an octave as the hunger in his eyes intensifies.

"I...do," I say, the need for this man's hands on my body making it difficult to think with any sort of clarity.

"I was hoping you didn't pay too much because I can't wait a second longer to get you naked."

His nostrils flare as he holds the camisole and tears it. I gasp, both shocked and delighted. The man does have a thing for tearing my clothes and I secretly love it.

"Oh," I say.

"If it was expensive, I'll replace it," he murmurs softly as he cups my breasts and bends to take my nipples into his mouth. I run my hands through his hair, and throw my head back as pleasure races through me.

"Not expensive," I whisper as he laves one nipple and pinches the other. Sensations race through me, settle between my legs. "That feels so good, Jamie." I hold his head to me, and he pushes a knee between mine, spreading me until I'm sitting on his leg. I grind myself on his thigh and his tortured growl pulls a chuckle from my throat. Truthfully, I love the way he wants me.

"Something funny?" he asks, as he kisses a path up my neck.

"Nothing funny," I say and ride his leg, rubbing and stimulating my clit, in ways that are making me delirious.

"You like torturing me, don't you?"

"I would never do that," I say as he kisses my ear, his breath hot on my flesh.

"Maybe I'll tie you to the bed and jerk off into my hands and make you watch."

I tremble. Almost violently.

Jamie laughs. "Like that idea, do you?"

"Yes, no, I don't know," I say, my mind on an erotic journey as I picture him doing just that.

He gives me a little shove and I fall to the bed. His grin is devilish as he tears into his shorts, and removes them, kicking them away. "Touch yourself," he commands in a soft voice.

He takes his cock into his big hand and strokes from the base to the crown. He grunts something I can't decipher, and when his gaze drops to the needy juncture between my legs, I slide the lace to one side to expose my pussy to him. "Finger yourself for me. Show me how you do it when you're alone."

I grin. Who knew Jamie was a true voyeur at heart? Not

me, but if he wants a show I'll give him one. I wet my lips and slide my fingers over my clit before I push them inside. A whimpering sound I have no control over escapes my lips, and with unabashed passion, I move my fingers in and out, growing hotter and wetter by the second.

"Yeah, baby, like that." He cups his balls and continues to rub his cock, the muscles on his arms tightening as he increases the speed. "I loved fucking you this week. Your mouth. Your tits, and your sweet hot pussy."

I moan as his nostrils flare with need. "But baby, I am going to take that virgin ass of yours tonight."

Cock still in his hand, he bends and grabs his shorts. He fumbles around in his pocket and pulls out a new tube of lube. I chuckle. "So this is why it took you so long to get back."

"I told you we'd fuck like this, but I needed you properly prepared, and we definitely need this."

I sit up, open the nightstand drawer and pull out an identical tube, and he shakes his head. "I do love a girl who knows what she wants."

He tosses the lube onto the bed, and goes to his knees on the floor. His lips find mine, and his kisses are soft, tender, and if I had to guess, born out of some deeper emotion. My heart beats faster with hope that we can have a future, that Jamie is ready to open up and take risks in life. But I'm not a risk. I love him. I've always loved him.

"Jamie," I say softly and his big hands trace my curves, a leisurely exploration. Tonight, there is no rush, no frenzied passion. No tonight, he's taking things slower, and that comes with its own ecstasy. He inches back and his breathing is labored.

"After tonight, I'll have been inside you, everywhere." I nod, and fall back onto the bed. "But first, I want your cum,

Fallon. I need to taste you." He touches my panties and pulls them down my legs.

"Yes, please," I say and catch the intensity in his eyes. I'm not sure I've ever seen this fierce, determined look on him before. What is going through his mind?

I want to ask, but lose all focus when he flattens himself on the bed beside me. "I want you to ride my mouth. I want you to take everything you need."

He holds my hands to balance me as I straddle his body. His hands slide up to my waist and he pulls me onto his mouth. As he lowers me, the soft blade of his tongue connects with my clit, and I let loose a loud moan.

"Ride me, baby. Come all over my face."

My clit swells and I grind down on him, rocking my hips like I'm a damn porn star as I give in to all the things this man makes me feel. I brace my hands on the headboard and slide against his mouth. He lifts me a bit and shoves his tongue inside me. My God, the man knows how to work my body.

My breath is ragged as his hands leave my hips to cup my ass cheeks and spread them. All week he's been playing with me a little. Stretching and preparing me for his girth. When he finally takes me like that, in a way no man ever has before, I know he's going to wreck me—in more ways than one.

He inserts his finger into my ass, and I back up against it, and rub my clit on his chin. I glance down, and it turns me on even more when I see how wet I've made his face.

I've come from clitoral stimulation before, but that was with the help of my vibrator, which is so not going to cut it after Jamie. I slide back, and his finger goes in further, and the bristles on his chin brush against my clit.

I rock, and move and grind and close my eyes to concentrate on the sweet, sweet pleasure. Beneath me his grunts and groans take me higher and higher, and my heart thuds a little harder, knowing how much he loves eating me and tasting my cum. He moves his finger inside my ass, and the full feeling rocks my world.

I go up on my knees as my muscles clench, a damn bursting inside me. He shoves a finger into my pussy, giving me something to clench down on, and it makes me come harder than I ever have before.

"Jamie," I cry out, shamelessly. "Fuck, Jamie," I say and he lifts his head to lick my clit, drawing out my pleasure. The spasms slow to a stop and he pulls his finger out and his tortured groan fills me with happiness as he drinks in my cum. He stays between my legs for a long time, and I take my breasts into my hands. I tug on my nipples, pinch them and roll them in my fingers.

"You're killing me, babe," Jamie says and that's when I realize he's been watching me touch myself.

I laugh, but it comes out more like a whimpering moan. Jamie sits up, spends some time with my nipples, then pushes forward until I'm on my back, my legs around him. His nostrils flare as his gaze moves over my face.

"You're the most beautiful woman I've ever set eyes on, Fallon," he says, so softly, so quietly and honestly, it curls around my body and hugs tight.

I touch his face. "Jamie," I say, and I'm about to tell him I love him when he presses his mouth to mine for a deep, tender kiss that tunnels into my heart and makes itself at home.

His lips slowly leave mine, and he carefully turns me over until my breasts are pressed into the mussed bedding. He cups my ass and squeezes. "Mine," he says. "All mine."

I swallow, and get the sense that taking me this way, marking me a way no one ever has, is affecting him in much the same way as it's affecting me.

"Lift," he says with a slight tap to my hip. I lift for him

and he puts a pillow beneath my hips. He spread me, runs his finger over my opening. "You want my cum in here?" he asks.

"I do, Jamie."

"Yeah, me too," he says, and I wiggle. He falls over me, his breath hot on my neck as he rips into the lube. "I need you nice and wet so it doesn't hurt. I want this to be good for you, babe."

"It will be because I'm with you," I say, wanting to be as honest with him as he is being with me.

"Yeah, same for me," he murmurs quietly.

Coolness invades my back as he inches away, taking his heat with him. I move a little on the pillow and go perfectly still when his cold, lubed finger touches me.

"Relax for me, baby."

I take a deep breath and let it out slowly and as I do, he slides his well-lubricated finger into my body. "Ooh," I say as the coldness gives way to heat. "Nice," I say.

He works me for a long time and one finger turns into two. I move my body, stimulate my clit on the pillow and soon enough arousal pulls at me once again.

"You ready for this?" he asks in a gruff voice full of need.

"I'm ready for you, Jamie."

He spreads me, and his cock presses against my opening as he grips my hips and pulls me back a bit. I'm wide open and vulnerable, but I'm not feeling fear. No, I've never been more excited, more eager for anything in my life.

His crown widens me even more and I fist the bedding at the sensation. He gives me another inch, and lightly strokes his fingers over my back, murmuring softly and giving me time to get used to the fullness. With excruciating slowness, he works his way into me, and the minutes tick by as he continues to take his time.

"I love seeing you like this," he murmurs. "Love the way your body is opening for me. I wish you could see what I see,

Fallon. Wish you could see my cock, and the way you're taking me." His voice breaks a bit when he adds, "You...you are so goddamn perfect."

"Jamie," I murmur and look over my shoulder to see him. Eyes heavy lidded, and latched onto my ass, he gives me a little more of his beautiful cock.

"I'm a wreck, baby. A total fucking wreck," he says, his voice hitching in a way I've never heard before.

The love I feel for this man curls through me, and tears prick my eyes. Never have I felt so deeply for another person. When he's just about all the way in, he stops, and his low deep groan, like he's working hard to keep it together, reaches my ears and curls around me.

I murmur and move my hips in encouragement. "I want it all, Jamie. Please...give me everything," I say and I get the sense he knows I'm asking for more than just his body.

His hips jerk forward, until he's filling me completely. "You've got all of me now," he whispers, and lightly strokes down my sides until he's gripping my hips. I go silent beneath him, struggling to get my emotions under control. "Are you good, Fallon?" he asks, easily reading me.

"I'm good," I manage to get out, and he moves his hips, sliding out a bit, and squeezes more lube onto my backside. He pushes in and the movement presses my clit to the pillow.

"Yes," I cry out.

One palm flattens on my back, and with the other still gripping my hip, he sinks into me. I move with him, slow easy movements, each giving and taking in a way that is more emotional, less physical. As our bodies join as one, and our moans merge, my muscles begin rippling again.

"Jamie, I'm coming," I cry out.

"I feel you," he says and moves a little quicker. As I let go, he lifts my hips higher, driving into me that much deeper and as he strokes my body, I explode with new sensations.

"Yessss," I hiss and tug at the sheets, tears of joy in my eyes thanks to this new experience.

"I'm there, Fallon. I'm right fucking there with you," he says in a soft voice that wraps around me like an old favorite blanket.

"Please fill me," I say and the next couple pumps are for him as his orgasm presses. He lets go on a growl and spurts high inside me. Warmth curls through my blood as he spasms so hard, it rockets through me and shatters me from the inside out.

He grunts loudly, falls over my back, and before I can stop myself, I whisper, "It should have been you."

Last night with Fallon...Jesus, I can't even put in to words what being with her like that did to me. The way she gave herself to me, trusting her body in my hands... Fuck, man. Totally blew my mind. Although she's been quiet most of today. Perhaps she's tired from a week in the sun, and all our late nights, or perhaps, like me, she's wondering where we go from here.

The truth is, I want to be the guy for her. I want to be everything she needs me to be. She might have said she didn't want to date again, but that night on the beach she admitted something different. In a perfect world she'd be happily married, with a loving trusting guy, one who could be a great father for Chase and put the needs of his family first.

I want to be that guy.

Is it possible that I can be? Is it possible that I can forgive myself for the accident—something Fallon assured me wasn't my fault—and allow myself to be happy again.

I glance up, and beneath the moonlight, Fallon is laughing and smiling as she gives everyone a good-bye hug, promising to meet the girls for coffee back in the city when they all return in a week. I haven't seen her this happy in a long time and it tugs at my heart to know I was the one who helped her find her way out of the darkness. Just like she's helping me.

"Hey bud," Cole says coming up beside me.

"Hey," I say, and toss the last of the bags into the back of the SUV.

"Back to the real world for you guys." I close the SUV and turn to Cole. "Nice to see you happy again."

I laugh. "I am happy," I say.

"She's good for you."

I look past his shoulder and my heart beats a little faster when Fallon walks toward me, a tired Chase dragging his feet beside her.

"You're good for her too, Jamie," Cole says. I nod in agreement, and Fallon gives Cole a hug when she reaches us.

"Thanks for inviting us. I had a wonderful week," she says.

"Now all you have to do is convince Jamie here to buy the Johnson property on the cove. Then you guys can come every year, and stay longer with us all."

She casts a glance my way, like she's gauging my reaction to that suggestion, and I know we definitely have to sit down and talk.

"Time to go home," I say to her. "You ready?"

She nods and buckles Chase into his car seat and circles the vehicle to slip into the passenger side. "Talk to you later, Cole. Thanks for the invite. We'll shoot some pool when you get back to the city," I say to him as I climb into the driver's seat. I start the vehicle, my heart so full of love for the woman beside me, as well as the boy in the back seat, it's a wonder I can even think. I back out of the driveway and soon enough we're on the highway. Fallon yawns.

"Tired?" I ask and slide my hand across the seat to capture hers.

"Yeah, you?"

"Too tired to have a talk when we get back?"

She sits up a little straighter. "No, I think it's a good idea." She gestures with a nod to Chase. "When little ears are asleep."

I chuckle and give her hand another squeeze, not wanting to let go. Ever. Fallon sinks back into her seat and hums softly to the song on the radio—thank God it's not that damn chomp, chomp alligator song—as I drive us home.

Home.

Man, I really like the sound of that. Her lids fall heavy beside me, and I lower the music, letting her drift off. Time slips by and as I pull onto our street, I notice the motion sensor floodlight over my garage is on. What the hell?

I had planned to take Fallon and Chase to their place, but I pull into my driveway to shine the lights onto the house, and Fallon stirs.

"We're here?" She rubs her eyes. "I'm sorry. I didn't mean to fall asleep."

I touch her leg as I scan the lawn and house, finding nothing out of the ordinary. "My motion sensor floodlight is on. It's probably nothing, but with the break-ins I should check it out."

"Are you sure you should go in?"

I glance into the back seat, and Chase is asleep. "I'll take you guys home first, then come back."

"No, we'll wait here. If anyone is in there, Jamie..."

"Okay, don't get out of the vehicle. Here are the keys. Lock up when I get out," I say. As an uneasy feeling prowls through my blood, I exit the vehicle and Fallon relocks the door. I step up to my garage, key in the code, and stand back as the double doors lift. My heart jumps into my throat when I find a little white Honda Civic parked beside my black truck.

No fucking way.

I glance back at Fallon, and squint against the headlights. Her door cracks open, because she knows exactly who is in my house. She slides out of the truck, and quietly closes her door, not wanting to wake Chase.

"Jamie," she says her voice shaking. "What's going on?"

"Your guess is as good as mine," I say and we both jump and turn at the sound of the front door banging open with a thud. Sara comes from the house, her steps a little wobbly as she grips the handrail and glares at us.

"Well isn't this sweet," she slurs.

"What are you doing, Sara?" I ask, my pulse pounding against my throat. After all this time, she just shows up? No calls, no texts, no communication for a year. Yes, I get that she hates me but to show up and get drunk?

She stumbles on the steps and I hurry to her before she falls and cracks her head open. I right her, and when she's finally stable, she shoves me away.

"What am I doing? What am I doing?" she shrieks, her voice bordering on hysteria.

"Sara," Fallon says in a calming voice that doesn't seem to have any effect on Sara. "We should go inside."

Sara snorts. "So what is this, Fallon? Tit for tat?" she asks, as her head bobs back and forth between the two of us.

"Sara," Fallon hisses. "Don't."

"Don't tell me what to do. You think because I needed time away that you could go to the beach with Jamie and fuck him."

"Sara, please. It's not what you think."

"What does she think?" I ask, totally confused by the tit for tat comment. "What is she talking about, Fallon?"

"I...just..."

"Fallon?" I ask, my stomach tightening. Jesus, what does she know that she's not telling me?

"I know she told you, Jamie," Sara says. "She hates me

enough, and sleeping with you, well, that was just payback. Isn't that right, Fallon?"

I back up, and stop when I land in my bushes. "Payback? Somebody better fucking tell me what's going on here."

Sara's eyes go wide, like she just had a revelation. "You're kidding me?"

"Sara, I never said—" Fallon begins but stops when Sara throws herself at me, and tears form in her eyes.

"Jamie, I've missed you," Sara cries.

What the fuck is going on?

I peel her arms from around my neck and set them at her side. "What are you talking about payback?"

"Nothing. I've been drinking." She blinks up at me, and tries to brush whatever this is, off. But I'm not about to let it go.

I turn to Fallon. "What is she talking about?"

"Jamie," she begins and reaches for me, but I avoid contact.

"Tell me, Fallon."

"Not here, Jamie. Not now."

"Shut your mouth," Sara says.

"Fallon, please..." I plead.

She takes a breath, lets it out slowly and lowers her head. "I'm sorry, Jamie."

"What are you sorry for?" I ask, as my gaze moves over her face, trying to read her.

"Sara and Ethan were having an affair. I was ninety-nine percent sure. Now I'm one hundred."

"You bitch," Sara says and launches herself at Fallon. She digs her nails into Fallon's arms, and scratches before I can pull her off. I drag her away, and she softens in my arms, changing tactics with me. "It was a mistake, Jamie. You were away a lot. I was lonely. It just happened."

I clench down on my teeth hard enough to break them.

I'm angry that Sara had an affair—with my brother, no less— but angrier that Fallon kept secrets from me. "You knew about this and didn't tell me?" I ask Fallon.

"Jamie," she says.

"This," I say and wave my hand back and forth between Fallon and me. "Was some kind of get even scheme?"

Her face goes white, and she takes a wobbly step back. "Do you really think so little of me, Jamie? You think I'd do something like that?"

I pinch the bridge of my nose and tear into Fallon. "You told me the accident wasn't my fault. You asked me to trust you, but you never told me why."

"The accident wasn't your fault," she says, and again with no explanation.

"Someone better tell me what the fuck is going on," I bark.

"Shut the fuck up, Fallon," Sara says and I put her behind my back to prevent her from attacking again.

"Sara had an ultrasound appointment," I begin, going over the events of the day. "I was late, so she asked Ethan. Sara told me herself that if I had been home the accident wouldn't have happened. How could I not blame myself after that?" My mind races, and when it slows again, I face Sara. "You did have on ultrasound appointment on that Wednesday, right?"

"What...oh...I, um."

I shake my head as she hedges.

"I think you had the dates mixed up, Jamie," Fallon says softly. "You admitted to me that you were only half-listening at the time."

"What were you doing with Ethan? Where were you going?"

"We were just...it was a nice day." She throws her hands up in the air. "We were going for a drive."

I squeeze my eyes shut for a second, unable to process

anything that I'm hearing. "You let me believe you had an appointment, and I was late, and that's why you were with Ethan. All this time, I thought I was responsible. I blamed myself, tortured myself and you let me, to cover up the affair."

"I can't remember. It was a traumatic time. We'd just lost our baby. Come on, Jamie. Let's go inside. I can make this right between us again," she says, and pushes her body against me, like sex will make this all go away.

"I couldn't move on." I fist my hair and tug. "I thought I let you down, and I couldn't move on, because...because I didn't want to let anyone else down. You let me believe, let me hurt, just to cover for yourself."

Sara blinks up at me. "I was going to end it."

"The baby," I say, and an anguished cry catches in Fallon's throat. I turn on her, and her chest rises with a big gulp of air. "Jesus fuck, you knew that too?" Hurt and angry and feeling like I've been raked raw inside, I begin to shake all over. "All this time you knew the baby wasn't mine, and never said a fucking word. Was this some kind of fucked up game you were playing with me, to get back at Sara and Ethan?" She opens her mouth but I'm too fucking furious—betrayed by everyone, Ethan included—to hear what she has to say. "Who are you?" I ask, and she backs up until she hits the SUV.

"You know who I am," she says quietly, her voice shaking as hard as her body.

"No, I don't," I shoot back.

"I'm sorry, Jamie."

"Sorry, for what?" I shoot back. "For sleeping with me, for keeping all this from me? Or are you sorry I found out."

"Sorry you found out," she whispers, and I can't believe what I'm hearing.

"Jamie, forget about her," Sara says and fawns all over me. "Let's go inside. I can make it all up to you."

Does she really think she can make things better with sex?

"You should go," I say as my world shatters around me. Again.

Sara gives me a pleading look. "Jamie, wait."

I turn to Fallon, a new burden heavy on my shoulders. "You should go," I repeat.

The keys rattle in her hands as she darts to the driver's side, and climbs into the vehicle.

I look back at Sara, my heart a million broken pieces. "You were having an affair with my brother, and you were having his baby. I guess I'm smart enough to know what you were doing in that car to make him go off the road."

Her eyes narrow to slit, anger now at the forefront. "You want to know the truth Jamie?" she spits out. "Your whole life you've been in love with her." She points her finger at the SUV. "It was always Fallon this, Fallon that. You even have her name tattooed on her back. Maybe I got tired of it. Maybe I fucked Ethan to get back at you. Maybe this really is all your fault."

Fallon backs out of the driveway, and as I stand there under the floodlight with Sara, disgusted as all the pieces are falling into place, I press my palms to my eyes until I see stars.

"I want you gone. Out of here tonight. But since you can't drive, I'll call you a cab. I'll put your car in the driveway, and don't even think about coming to my door tomorrow when you pick it up." Sara pounds on my chest as I pull my phone from my back pocket. I call a cab, and set her on the front steps as I drive her car out of the garage. Then I grab her arm and march her to the end of the driveway until the cab comes. I put Sara into the back seat, and send her away with it.

Feeling a little lost, and a whole lot angry, I head inside and bang around as I make my way to the kitchen. I take a beer from the fridge, swallow half the contents in one gulp, and pull my phone out again as I stalk into the living room.

I call Cole at his beachside cottage, he answers on the second ring. "Did you fucking know?" I ask, getting right to the point.

"Know what?" he asks. A door slams and I'm guessing he's gone into another room for privacy. "What's going on?"

"Did you know Sara was fucking Ethan and the baby was his?"

A beat of silence, and then, "Jesus fuck, I'm sorry to hear that Jamie, and I'm also sorry to say it doesn't surprise me. But if I knew something like that, don't you think I'd tell you?" he shoots back.

"Exactly. Just like Fallon should have told me."

I hear a rustling sound in the background, and Huxley barking. "Back it up, tell me what's going on."

"That night by the fire, you said there were things I didn't know. If you didn't know my brother and my fiancée were fucking around, what things were you talking about?"

"Oh, fuck." I grip my phone and Cole takes a deep breath and lets it out slowly. "Ethan was your brother, and he's gone. I don't want to talk badly about him, but Jamie, as his big brother, *his protector*, there are so many things you overlooked, or didn't really see at all."

I lean forward, brace my elbows on my legs. "What are you talking about?"

"You and Fallon. You two always belonged together. If everyone else saw it, Ethan had to have seen it too. He wanted her because you wanted her."

A storm roils through me as I mull that over. "I backed off because...because he was my kid brother and I would have done anything in the world for him."

"I know this is going to hurt, but that didn't go both ways. Ethan always wanted to outshine you. I don't know why. I wasn't there to see the dynamics when you two were growing up."

I think back to all Ethan's antics, all the risks he'd took, stunts he pulled, to get the adoration and approval of everyone around him. Was that to outshine me?

"Maybe he didn't like that you were better at hockey, that you were adored by so many."

"Ethan never liked hockey. He never went to a single game of mine. Never even put Chase in skates."

"But you watched him race, right?"

The knot in my stomach tightens. "Whenever I could."

Ethan was jealous of me? Wanted to outshine me?

"I can't say where the envy comes from. Maybe he was just hardwired that way." A beat of silence, and then, "That's why I'm not surprised to hear he went after Sara."

My heart aches in my constricted tight chest as my thoughts go to Fallon's betrayal. Trust is important to me, she of all people knows that. "Fallon knew everything."

"Yeah."

"She kept it from me. Said she was sorry I found out."

"Why would she keep that from you?"

"Sara said it was payback. Tit for tat." A humorless laugh escapes my throat. "She slept with Ethan so Fallon was getting even by sleeping with me."

"Fallon slept with you because she loves you, Jamie. One look at you two and it's easy to tell how crazy you are about each other."

"Sara said something like that."

Fuck me.

"Maybe there were other reasons she kept it from you," Cole says.

"Like what?"

"Maybe you've been through enough, and she didn't want to see you hurt anymore. You're a protector at heart, always protecting your little brother, and maybe she was protecting you from him."

"You think?"

"You'll have to ask her, but yeah, I think."

"She said she was ninety-nine percent sure of the affair, until Sara pretty much confirmed it."

"That could be another reason she didn't tell you. She has great intuition, but maybe she didn't have proof."

Is it possible that Cole is right, that she kept that from me because, one, she wasn't sure, and two, she was protecting me? Christ, if so, I totally fucked everything up between us. The hurt look on her face, the way she fled after I told her to go. There's no coming back from that. She should hate me. Fuck, I hate myself.

I grip my hair and tug. "I accused her of playing some fucked-up game with me." The look on her face was pure devastation when she asked if that was what I thought of her.

Cole groans. "Shit."

"Yeah." A lump fills my throat, and pain spreads to my jaw, then settles at the base of my neck where a headache begins brewing. "Oh fuck, man, the hurtful things I said to her."

"You were angry. She's smart enough to realize you were striking out in the moment."

"I fucking hurt her, Cole." I stand, and pace to the window, catch a glimpse of her SUV as she drives back down our street, slowing to see the white Honda still in my drive-way. Where the hell is she going? I need to go after her. "I really hurt her."

"Then make it right."

"How?"

"You're a smart guy. You'll figure it out." Just then my doorbell rings and my heart leaps. "Maybe that's her," Cole says.

"Gotta go," I say and disconnect the call.

I hurry to the door, pull it open and find my father on the steps. "Dad," I say and look past his shoulders, but the SUV is long gone. "Did you pass Fallon?"

He nods. "She called me. She told me Sara had been here, and wanted me to call to make sure you were all right. I thought I'd come by instead."

"She...called you?"

"She was pretty worried about you."

After the cruel things I said, she called my Dad? Was worried about me?

I have no idea why that surprises me. Fallon is kind, caring, and always puts the best interests of others first. Which, of courses, was why she didn't tell me her suspicions about the affair, or the baby. She was protecting me, goddammit.

I am such a fucking idiot.

"I hurt her," I say, and sink to my knees in the front foyer as my heart gallops in my chest.

"Let's talk," Dad says.

I take a few deep breaths, push to my feet and eventually follow him into the living room. "Do you know where she is?" I ask.

"No, she didn't say."

"I love her, Dad."

"I know you do," he says with a nod.

"Do you hate me for that?"

"Son, you've always loved her. Everyone knew that."

"That's what Cole said." I consider that a moment longer and ask a question I'm not sure I want the answer too. "Do you think...Ethan knew how I felt about her?"

He scrubs the bristles on his chin, looks off into the distance, and gives a small nod. "Yes."

That one word, and the honesty behind it, takes the air from my lungs. I sit there, stars dancing in my brain like I'd just been body-checked against the boards. As I look at my dad, take in the lines around his eyes, think about the pain and suffering he endured at losing a son, my eyes fill with tears.

No way am I about to tell him Sara and Ethan were having an affair and the baby was his. There are some things he doesn't need to know. Not only do I not want to hurt him, I want to protect the memory of his son. Like Cole said, I'm a protector at heart. So is Fallon.

Yeah, Fallon not telling me. I totally get it now.

"I need to make things right," I say, fighting down the panic that I might not be able to do that. That it might be too late.

My dad stands, and I climb to my feet. As we stand eye to eye, he puts his hand on my shoulder. "Are you okay, son?"

"No, I'm not. I haven't been okay in a long time. But I'm really hoping I will be soon."

15

FALLON

Last night after my run-in with Sara, and the cruel thing Jamie accused me of, there was no way I could go back into my house and sleep. Not after sharing the place with Ethan, and then playing house with Jamie. With Chase asleep in the back of the SUV, I went for a drive and somehow found myself at the graveyard. A visit was something I'd been wanting to do since arriving back in Seattle. At Ethan's resting spot, I sat there for a very long time, going over the events of the past year, and the months before his death.

Even though I'm not a religious person, I said a few prayers, for Ethan and the baby, and since holding on to old hurts is far too hard on my head, I let everything go in that instant. With tears in my eyes, I climbed back into my vehicle and drove around for a very long time, until exhaustion pulled at me and I went home, and then I tucked Chase into his bed, and I went back to the spare room that I hadn't been sleeping in with Jamie.

I stared at the ceiling most of the night...wondering. Had Sara convinced Jamie to take him back? Had Jamie forgiven her? Her car was still in the driveway well into the wee hours of the morning when I returned home. I want Jamie to be happy, and if Sara makes him happy then so be it. Hopefully she'll have learned from past mistakes and they can move on —much like I plan to move on.

But how can I do that without Jamie—the man I loved for as long as I can remember. I'm not sure but I'll have to find a way. My heart squeezes in my too tight chest, and filling my lungs is much more difficult. For a time last night, I thought about running again. Going back to my mother's in Spokane, but that's not fair to Chase. His uncle might be angry at me, might want me out of his life for good, but I can't imagine that would extend to Chase.

A pounding sound reverberates through my head. At first I think it's a headache, but then I realize it's Chase running down the hall. I kick off the blankets, and note that he'd slept in. He was probably exhausted from a long week at the beach, and broken sleep in the SUV last night.

"I'm coming, bud," I say and look at myself in the mirror as I rise. Wow, I hope someone got the license plate of the truck that ran me over. I smooth my hand over my mess of hair but other than a bucket of makeup, there is nothing I can do about the black smudges beneath my eyes.

"I want pancakes," Chase yells as he darts into the bathroom.

My throat tightens. Pancakes were his and Jamie's thing.

"Okay. I'll make them for you."

"I want Jamie to make them," he says.

So do I.

My heart squeezes. Chase had gotten so used to Jamie being here and then poof, he's out of his life one morning just like that. That wasn't fair of me. I should have been more careful.

"Not today, kiddo. But you can help me with the batter."

He comes from the bathroom with a pout on his face. "Where's Jamie?"

Keep it together, girl.

"He's busy. But I'm here to help." When he looks like he's about to protest I say, "I think I have some chocolate chips we can sprinkle in."

"Chocolate chips," he yells, and darts down the stairs a million miles an hour.

He reaches the kitchen before me, and as I walk down the hall, my doorbell rings. I go perfectly still, my heart in my throat.

Could it be?

I turn directions, walk slowly to the door, and take a breath and hold it as I swing it open. But it's not Jamie on my stoop. Nope, it's Jamie's parents and they both have strange expressions on their faces. Worry creeps through me.

"Is Jamie okay?" I ask quickly.

"Jamie is fine," Barry says.

Then what is going on? Why are they at my place Saturday morning before noon?

I think back to last night. I called Barry, told him Sara had returned and suggested he call his son. I wanted him to check in with Jamie, just to make sure he was okay. But what exactly did Jamie tell him? Could they know about the affair, the baby...about us? If so are they angry?

Marion speaks and that's when I realize I've been standing there thinking. "I'm sorry. Please come in. What's going on?" I ask cautiously.

"We thought you and Chase might like to go for a drive today."

"I don't think—"

"Mommy, I want to go," Chase says coming from the kitchen. Marion opens her arms, and he runs into them.

"You're house hunting, aren't you? John called this morning with the perfect house for you. He said you had to act fast, though."

"Why did he call you and not me?"

She shakes her head. "Well, isn't that a good question." She claps her hands. "Nevertheless, we need to get going."

"I'm not even dressed."

"I was making pancakes, Grandma," Chase says, and my heart beats a little faster as he beams up at his grandparents.

"How about we go through the drive thru and get you pancakes on our way to look at the house?"

"Can we, Mommy?"

"I guess so," I say, my head spinning as this is all coming so fast at me.

Chase and I dart upstairs, we wash, dress, and brush our teeth, and back downstairs, Marion and Barry are talking quietly. They part quickly when they see us, and I angle my head.

"Is everything okay?"

"Everything will be okay," Barry says. "At least that's what I've been told."

Not understanding his cryptic words, we head outside, and Barry insists he drive. Since the car seat is in the SUV, I climb in back with Chase and give the passenger seat up to Marion.

We go through a fast food drive through and we all get something to eat. With my head down, I help Chase with his pancakes, but we both end up a sticky mess in the end anyway. When I finally lift my head, I glance around.

"Where are we going? Where is this place? I wanted to be in the city, closer to the hospital."

"I wonder if John misunderstood," Marion says, keeping her eyes straight ahead.

"I don't want to live this far out," I say, and wonder what's really going on here. They both ignore me from the front seat, and I realize too late where they're taking me. "Why are we headed to Wautauga Beach?"

"Perhaps John found something here for you," Barry says.

I sit back, and stare out the window, chaos erupting in my stomach. Barry and Marion are up to something, of that I'm certain. We drive a little while longer, and they pull into the driveway of the Johnsons' cottage. Jamie and Cole had viewed it shortly after we arrived, but I was too busy with Chase to join them. But this place is too big for us and too far out for a daily commute. Besides, I could never live here. Everyday I'd be reminded of Jamie, and what I'd loved and loss.

"Mommy, we're at the beach," Chase says and sits up a bit straighter. "There's Huxley." He points as Cole, Nina, and Brandon come our way. Behind them I see all the others, but Jamie is nowhere to be found. Not that I expected he'd come back here.

I open my door slowly, and the warm sun shines down on us as everyone comes to greet us. "What's going on, Cole?" I ask, and he just smiles at me and points a finger toward the front door of the Johnsons' cottage.

My heart jumps into my throat and I sink to my knees, tears in my eyes. "What...what are you doing?" I ask so quietly there is no way Jamie can hear me from where he's standing at the top of the stairs.

"Mommy, Mommy," Chase says, and Nina goes to his side of the car and lets him out.

Barry reaches for me, and helps me to my feet. "I'm sorry we tricked you. But I'm not really," he says with a grin. "John did think this place was good for you. We all do. You and Jamie deserve this."

"What are you saying?" I ask.

"Never mind what I have to say. Go see what Jamie has to say." He turns me and gives me a little nudge. I walk toward the stairs and Jamie comes toward me. That's when I realize he's holding a dog.

"Jamie?" I ask.

He smiles at me, and calls out, "Chase."

Chase comes running up and Jamie drops to his knees. "This guy is for you."

Chase's eyes go so wide I think they're going to fall out of his head as he looks at the mutt. "It's not a Huxley. Actually, he's a rescue dog, and he needs someone to love him."

He hands the dog over, and Chase and everyone starts to laugh as the dog gives big wet kisses.

"You can name him whatever you like. But probably not Huxley, since we have a Huxley already," Jamie says as the dog stops licking and starts chomping on the sleeve of Chase's T-shirt.

"I'm going to call him Chomp," Chase says, and Huxley comes over and starts sniffing the pup.

"Great, more reminders of the alligator song," Jamie says with a hard roll of his eyes.

"I think he likes you, Chase." I stand back up as Chase sets the dog down and starts running around, little Chomp and Huxley running after him.

"I think I like you, Fallon," Jamie says softly, his thumb under my chin, bringing my face to his.

"On that note," Cole says loudly. "Let's all go for a walk. Come on, Chase."

Knowing my son is in good hands, I let him go, and face the man I love. "Jamie, what is all this?" I ask, and look at the cottage behind him. "Did you buy this place?"

"Yes, for us."

"For us?" I manage to get out as my throat tightens.

"This is my way of telling you how fucking sorry I am and showing you just how much I love you." I draw in a breath of happiness as my love for him floods my heart. His fingers graze mine as he continues. "I was a complete ass last night. I said terrible things, Fallon." He swallows hard. "I was hurt, confused…I didn't understand why you would keep things from me." He pulls me close, presses a kiss to my forehead. "But I know now. I understand, and I'm here to prove I can be the man you need, and I want to give you that perfect world, Fallon. You deserve it. I deserve it too. Forgive me, please."

I smile at that, so happy to see his wounds healing. "Jamie, you were a wreck before I came back, and over the past few weeks, you became the man you used to be, the man I've always loved."

"You've always loved me?" he asks, his dark eyes half lidded, full of so love and hope, and life…something I hadn't seen in them for a long time.

"Yes, and I wasn't sure if I was right about Sara and Ethan. Even if I was right, I wasn't sure I wanted to tell you. But I couldn't let you keep blaming yourself either. I was so torn. When I said I was sorry that you found out, I meant it. I was sorry. I was sorry for what two people you really cared about did to you."

"To you, too."

"I know. But I was really sorry you found out the way you did. Getting blindsided like that. That wasn't fair, Jamie."

He shakes his head. "We all know life isn't fair. But life does go on, and I want to go on—with you at my side." He pulls something from his back pocket and drops to one knee.

A gasp catches in my throat and tears blur my vison. "Jamie."

"I love you too, Fallon. I've always loved you. I want to make a life with you. I want to summer here with you and our friends. I want Chase to be my son. I want to be a father to him. I want us to get that small house in the city by the hospital and good schools, like you want. Please say yes to all of this."

I stare at the man I love, and as he looks up at me with hopeful eyes, I shake my head no.

"Fallon," he says, still on his knees, his breath a little faster, a new urgency in his voice. "Tell me what I need to do to make this right. You're my best friend, the woman I love. I can't lose you. I can't. I can't be whole without you."

I fall to my knees with him and cup his face. "I can't say yes to all those things, because I don't want a small house with you. I want a big house, with a lot of bedrooms so we can fill them with children, children made and born from our love."

Water pools in his eyes as he slides his hand around my neck and pulls me in for a soul-searing kiss. "I love you, Fallon."

"I love you too," I say.

"Chase will always have his daddy in heaven, but I can't wait to tell him I can be like a daddy."

"You're going to be a great daddy," I say and press my lips to his for another tender kiss.

When we ease a part he grins and says, "And I'm getting that boy in a pair of skates asap."

I laugh at that. "Yeah you are."

He takes the ring from the box, and I hold my hand out to him. He slides it on, kisses me again and turns to our family and friends, who are hovering pretty close by.

"She said yes!"

Jamie and I both let loose a loud laugh as everyone starts clapping and jumping and come running our way. Jamie turns back to me, and cups my face.

"We can find our normal now, babe."

"Together we can find everything," I assure him. He's about to stand, but I stop him. I press my lips to his again, and seductively whisper, "Thanks, Jamie." He pins me with a heated look and the needy growl that follows thrills me to my core, and I know we're going to have a life full of love, happiness, and a lot of thankfulness.

AFTERWORD

Thank You!

Thank you so much for reading The Risk Taker, book five in my Players on Ice series. I hope you enjoyed the story as much as I loved writing it. Please read on for an excerpt of Confessions of a Bad Boy Professor. Stay turned for more Players on Ice.

Interested in leaving a review? Please do! Reviews help readers connect with books that work for them. I appreciate all reviews, whether positive or negative.

Happy Reading,
Cathryn

BAD BOY PROFESSOR

Justin

Another weekend. Another party.

I need to give this shit up.

I swirl the amber liquid in my glass and glance around the bar to take in the group of loud girls partying around me. I try to find the one I'd just danced for in a private party room off the main bar. I'm not really sure why I'm looking for her. She's just another girl in a sea of women I dance for once in a while.

My gaze lands on her, sitting at the other end of the bar, uncomfortable, nervous and so goddamn beautiful my dick swells.

Okay, maybe I do know why I'm looking for her. I've been doing this gig for a long fucking time, and none of the girls I danced for were ever like her. The guys and I started dancing at parties to for cash when we were in college, and well, maybe my reasons had more to do with rebellion than money. The business flourished and spread to other states, and even though none of us need the money, we now dance when we have to fill in, or for kicks. But I'm tired of flying around, putting on a mask and shaking my cock in some drunk girl's face. But this girl, well, she's been nursing a drink for the last hour, and doesn't seem at all like the kind who would enjoy a half naked guy shaking his junk at her.

I catch her gaze, and hold it for a minute. She quickly turns away and my cock swells at her shyness. Shit. She's way too young and innocent for me. I have no idea what her story is or why her friends would hire me to dance for her twenty-first birthday, and I should leave it at that. If I knew what would good for me, I would.

But, fuck it. I rarely go with what's good for me, which is why I'm sitting on a goddamn bar stool in Virginia sipping on a scotch when I should be back at Penn State, grading papers. I'm bored with that job, too. But dear old dad is the dean, and while I had different career aspirations, both he and mom pushed me into education—hence my rebellious stage.

I swallow the rest of the liquid, let it burn its way down my throat. I don't normally stay for a drink after a gig, but tonight, I don't know, there's something about the birthday girl that's throwing me off. I pick up the backpack at my feet, the one stuffed with my dance clothes and mask, a necessity for me now. I'm a fucking psych professor, for Christ's sakes. Ever hear of a code of conduct? Yeah, well, I'm violating every rule I promised to uphold.

I really need to give this shit up.

I toss the bag over one shoulder and stand. The heat in the room, as well as the mixed scent of alcohol and perfume, washes over me. I'm anxious to get the hell out of here. Looks like the recipient of my dance is, too.

I push through the lively crowd, and slide in beside her at the bar. Her body goes stiff, and shit, I'm pretty sure I'd do anything to help her relax.

"Hey," I say.

She nibbles her bottom lip. Sexy as hell.

Fuck me.

I shift, and lean on the bar so she can't see my swelling cock.

"Hi," she says.

"Not really your scene, is it?"

She crinkles her nose. "Am I that obvious?"

"Yeah, a little bit." I take a glance around. "Want to get out of here? Walk the beach?"

Her back stiffens, and her chest juts out, her lovely nipples pressing against the silk of her blouse. "I don't even know you."

It's true. She doesn't. I was in costume when I danced for her, so no way can she know I'm the guy her friends hired to shake it in her face. I take in her wide blue eyes. So fucking innocent she's killing me.

Desperate to put her at ease, I shrug. "I don't know you either. How do I know once we're outside you won't try to get me out of my clothes and have your way with me?"

She smiles, and it rocks my fucking world. "I really could use some fresh air..."

I pick up on her hesitation. "Pass me your phone."

What the fuck am I doing?

Breaking all kinds of rules tonight, that's what I'm fucking doing.

"Why do you want my phone?" she asks as she slides it across the sticky bar top.

I hold it up, and take a selfie. "There, now you have my picture. If I try anything you don't like, you'll have my mug shot for the police."

She looks at me like I'm a bit insane. Maybe I am, because I should really leave this alone. She reaches for her purse, and I say, "Do you need to tell a friend?"

Her gaze flickers to the dance floor, but none of her friends are paying any attention to her. Girls are supposed to look out for one another when partying—come together and go together. But it doesn't look like she's made that pact with any of these drunk party girls. She frowns, a hint of loneliness ghosting her eyes, and my heart squeezes. At least she's in good hands with me. She's sweet and innocent and I don't—okay I do, but won't—want anything more from her than a conversation.

"Yeah, let's get out of here," she says.

"Wait." I pull out my phone and take a picture of her. "There, now if you try anything I don't like, I'll have your mug shot."

She blinks, surprised and I put my hand on the small of her back and guide her out the door. The night air is warm, sticky, but it's a break from the heat and bodies inside. I breathe deeply as the waves laps against the sand in the distance.

"I'm Justin, by the way."

"Violet."

Pretty, just like her.

The music becomes faint as we remove our shoes and step onto the sand. She exhales and runs the warm grains between her painted toes. *Painted toes*. Fuck, that's sexy, too.

Don't go there, dude.

"Can I ask a question?"

Her long curls bounce around her face and she purses her pouty, heart-shaped mouth as her big blue eyes meet mine. "You can ask, but it doesn't mean I'll answer."

Beautiful and funny.

A dangerous combination.

She doesn't know I'm the guy who danced for her, so I need to word my question carefully. "What were you doing at the bar? It doesn't seem like it's your kind of scene."

"It's not really. I work with those girls. We're not close, so I guess that's how they thought I should celebrate my twenty-first birthday."

"I've only known you for five minutes and I would never throw you a party like that."

"No? Then what would you do?" she asks.

I take in her skirt, the sleeveless silk blouse she has tucked into the hem, and say, "Quiet dinner, walk on the beach."

"You can tell all that from looking at me."

"Gut feeling." I'm not about to tell her I'm a psychology professor and study behavior and mind. Her behavior tonight told me everything I needed to know. She's a good girl, and I need to stay away.

She arches a brow. "You're pretty intuitive."

"You're beautiful." Shit. I hadn't meant to say that. Fucking just slipped out. I don't want her to think I'm coming on to her. She turns from me, and looks at the water. I'm pretty sure she's about to run the other way. I'm a stranger, eight years older than her, and I'm probably coming off like a stalker.

"Race you to the water," she says, and takes off. "Last one there has to go skinny dipping."

Skinny dipping?

I stand still for a moment, processing that as her skirt flies around her backside and she darts to the waves. She's not the kind of girl to go skinny-dipping, of that I'm certain. My brain kicks in and I chase after her. When I catch her, she's laughing and breathless.

Jesus fuck, the sound goes straight through me, and zaps what little control I seem to have around her. I touch her face, my thumb sweeping across her cheek. Her laugh dies and her eyes go wide as they latch onto mine.

"Violet."

"Yeah?"

"I really want to kiss you."

A moment of hesitation, then, "Okay."

I step into her, meshing my hardness with her softness. Sweet fuck, my cock grows another inch, and she gives a little gasp when she feels it. "Sorry," I say, but somehow I'm not. I actually want her to know she's beautiful, see what she does to me. I dip my head, and softly, lightly brush my lips over hers, not wanting to hurry the moment I might never have again.

A moan escapes her throat and I slide my hand to the back of her neck as I increase the pressure. I push my tongue in and we tangle. I catch the taste of the syrupy drink she'd been nursing, but it's not nearly as sweet as her. I close my eyes, savor, enjoy, drown in her flowery scent and taste. I'm only half aware as her hands snake around my back, her questing fingers splaying, touching, exploring my body.

I want to do the same.

Using slow movements so as not to scare her, I sweep my hands lower, run my fingers along her vertebrae until I'm at the small of her back. The sweet curve of her ass calls out to me. I dare to go lower and cup her roundness, and massage lightly as I pull her against my cock.

A sound lodges in her throat as she breaks from the kiss. I pull my hands away, and take in the flush on her cheeks as wide eyes stare up at me. Okay, now I've gone to far. She's going to run.

"You lost," she says on a breathless whisper.

Her words are a jumbled mess in my lust-filled brain. "Lost?"

"The race."

It only takes a second for my thoughts to catch up. Holy fuck. Is she serious?

Here I thought she was going to bolt, only for her to be staring at me, waiting for me to shed my clothes.

Fine, I'll play it her way

Pinterest http://www.pinterest.com/catkalen/

Hands On

Body Contact

Full Exposure

Dossier

Private Reserve

House Rules

Under Pressure

Big Catch

Brazilian Fantasy

Improper Proposal

Boys of Beachville

Good at Being Bad

Igniting the Bad Boy

Bad Girl Therapy

Stone Cliff Series:

Crashing Down

Wasted Summer

Love Lessons

Wrapped Up

Eternal Pleasure Series

Instinctive

Impulsive

Indulgent

Sun Stroked Series

Seaside Seduction

Deep Desire

Private Pleasure

Captured and Claimed Series:

Yours to Take

Yours to Teach

Yours to Keep

Firefighter Heat Series

Fever

Siren

Flash Fire

Playing For Keeps Series

Slow Ride

Wild Ride

Sweet Ride

Breaking the Rules:

Hold Me Down Hard

Pin Me Up Proper

Tie Me Down Tight

Stand Alone Title:

Hands on with the CEO

Torn Between Two Brothers

Holiday Spirit

Unleashed

Knocking on Demon's Door

Web of Desire

www.ingramcontent.com/pod-product-compliance
Lightning Source LLC
Chambersburg PA
CBHW021147190726
48288CB00008B/2871